D1190740

J.J.E.

JESSIE JANE EDWARDS

Judge, Juror and Executioner

Del,

It is a great honor to be your partner. It's an even greater honor to be your friend. All my best

Matthew Imes

authorHOUSE®

AuthorHouse™
1663 Liberty Drive
Bloomington, IN 47403
www.authorhouse.com
Phone: 833-262-8899

This is a work of fiction. All of the characters, names, incidents, organizations, and dialogue in this novel are either the products of the author's imagination or are used fictitiously.

Published by AuthorHouse 11/30/2021

ISBN: 978-1-6655-4409-2 (sc)
ISBN: 978-1-6655-4408-5 (e)

Print information available on the last page.

This book is printed on acid-free paper.

ACKNOWLEDGEMENT

W riting J.J.E. was in some ways more satisfying, and other ways more challenging than "What If?". I certainly enjoyed the process tremendously, and that process involves many more people than I can thank here. I do want to thank my wife for her thoughts and wonderful ideas as to how to give Jessie the best story possible. I also want to thank my agent, Lisa Darden, for her hard work and dedication to this project. I know I would not be where I am without such wonderful people in my life.

I also want to thank all the people who supported "What If?" and hope you enjoy this book as much as my first. Peace and love to you all.

CHAPTER 1

"Thank you for joining Action News 7 this evening. My name is Tracy Thomas and our top story today is the acquittal of Senator Lawrence Guidry on murder charges related to the death of his wife, Margaret. Reporter Bobby Prestridge is live at the courthouse in downtown New Orleans. Bobby, can you fill us in on the details?"

"Good evening, Tracy. There's quite a raucous crowd here, clearly surprised by the verdict. The police have placed barricades along the bottom of the steps for security purposes. We're waiting for comments from both the District Attorney's office, as well as from Senator Guidry's legal team."

Holding a hand to his ear, the reporter looked over his shoulder, "Wait a minute, it looks like the District Attorney is approaching the podium." The camera shifted to a close-up of the podium where a distinguished-looking gentleman in a navy suit stepped up to the bank of microphones.

"Good evening. I'm District Attorney Frank Simmons and I'll make a short statement before taking a few questions."

Removing notes from his jacket, he continued, "We are very disappointed with the outcome today. We strongly believed we had a good case against Senator Guidry and put forth our evidence in the best possible manner. Clearly things didn't go our way, but that said, the legal process has now been exhausted. Senator Guidry was found not guilty and there is no appealing the verdict. We would like to thank the jury for completing their civic duty over these past weeks."

DA Simmons put aside the notes and continued, "I would especially like to thank our team for all of the work that went into this case. It's never easy to prosecute a public official, but I've never been more proud of our staff than I am today. We worked tirelessly over the past year to make sure we did everything professionally, thoroughly and by the book. I would love to be in front of you right now speaking about a conviction, but we were unable to convince the jury of our position."

The DA leaned forward, staring intently into the crowd. "Let me be very clear. Senator Guidry has been found not guilty, he is a free man and is no longer subject to any criminal proceedings. Like or dislike the verdict, the Senator is not guilty under the rules of our justice system. Questions?"

Numerous hands went up with some people shouting questions before DA Simmons cut them off, "I won't answer any questions asked without permission. Marcy, go ahead with your question."

"Thank you, sir. What do you feel caused the jury to come back with the not guilty verdict?

"I don't know. We haven't had time to interview the jurors and I don't want to speculate. Tony?"

"Why did your office choose to seek a charge of first-degree murder, instead of a lesser charge?"

"Good question, Tony. In our opinion, the evidence clearly showed intent, and since intent is the trigger for a first-degree murder charge, we were determined to follow the law."

The camera shifted back to the Action News 7 reporter, "Tracy, we'll keep following the press conference and provide an update later in the newscast."

"Thank you, Bobby. In studio, we have Mark Martin, a retired court of appeals judge. Judge Martin, what do you make of the verdict?"

"Thanks for having me. I must admit, it's a bit of a head scratcher. I was in the courtroom for the entire trial. It's obvious to me the prosecutors met their burden of proof. That said, strange things can happen when the jury deliberates. We may never know what took place during the deliberation process, but I suspect some of the jurors will write books about it given the high profile of the case."

"Judge, do you feel a first-degree murder charge was appropriate?"

"I do. The prosecutors were able to clearly show intent."

Tracy steepled her fingers, "But wouldn't they have been more likely to get a conviction if they had settled on a lesser charge?"

The judge took a deep breath before responding. "The problem with that line of thought is where does it end? It's one thing if you choose a lesser charge when you have a questionable case, but as a prosecutor, you can't reduce charges on solid cases just to get a guilty verdict. If everyone did that, then a lot of criminals would not be punished appropriately for their crimes."

"I see," Tracy said before asking, "If you were on the jury, would you have voted guilty?"

With an affirmative nod, the judge replied, "Absolutely."

Tracy looked to her left and then back at the camera. "I've just been told Senator Guidry and his team are approaching the podium. We will now return to the courthouse."

Viewers once again saw the podium. Behind it were three people: two men and one woman. The woman approached and began to speak. "My name is Sarah Benoit. I'm the lead attorney for Senator Guidry. Obviously, we are pleased with the verdict. We would like to thank the jury for looking past the ugly rhetoric and for closely examining the facts of the case. It was clear to us from day one the prosecutors were mainly interested in smearing Senator Guidry's good name for political purposes. The killer is still at large and we call on the police to continue pursuing the investigation. Senator Guidry's family won't be able to rest until justice is done."

Sarah looked at Senator Guidry with a slight nod of her head before continuing, "Senator Guidry would like to say a few words."

Hisses and boos could be heard by the television viewers as the Senator approached the microphones. Holding his hands up for silence, he waited for a moment before speaking. "I'd like to thank my legal team for their outstanding work in my defense. I'd also like to thank the jury for being brave and confirming my innocence, despite the pressure being applied by outside interest groups."

Senator Guidry leaned forward and lowered his voice slightly. "My family will not stop looking until we find the real killer." He leaned back, slammed his fist into the podium and practically yelled, "Justice will be served!"

And with that, Senator Guidry grabbed his chest and collapsed. Pandemonium ensued with police and medical personnel rushing to assist, the crowd pressing forward to see what happened and the reporters all smelling a great story.

Had anyone turned to look away from the steps, they would have seen a woman walking slowly away. Nobody could have provided a detailed description about the lady because of the large sunglasses covering her face. What they would have been able to say is she had blond hair, was trim, well-dressed, walked with a purpose and never looked back.

CHAPTER 2

Waking in a cold sweat with tears running down my face had become too common an occurrence. Once again, sleep was disrupted by one of my recurring nightmares. In it, it's my birthday, and the present for turning 11 was the death of my mother.

The dream begins with me running downstairs on the morning of my special day, excited to see what my parents were going to do. Before reaching the bottom of the stairs, I knew something was wrong. I heard a strange man's voice coming from the living room, speaking in a hushed tone. Rounding the corner, I saw a policeman standing in the middle of the room, and my father sitting head in hands on the couch, crying.

When Dad heard me enter the room, he jumped up to hug me saying, "It'll be okay," over and over. I burst into tears, not knowing why. This is the point where I wake up each time I have the dream. And it's been happening more and more frequently over the years. The accident was 23 years ago, but it still feels like it happened yesterday.

In real life, Mom was killed when a drunk driver ran a red light and t-boned her. He was driving a huge SUV, and my mom's Toyota Corolla never stood a chance. The driver was arrested and charged with DUI and vehicular homicide. Fortunately for him, but not for us, the driver was an appellate court judge. The charges against him were dismissed due to a technicality, which I didn't understand at the time. When I grew up, I realized "technicality" was more properly called "privilege". My life was forever altered without the son-of-a-bitch having to suffer any repercussions. I don't care what others think, I had first-hand knowledge of how much our criminal justice system sucks.

Tears drying on my face, I crawled out of bed. Looking in the bathroom mirror, I saw my tired and haunted grey eyes looking back at me. I was going to have to do some serious work to get ready for the day.

My first stop was to Mom's grave. Fresh flowers in hand, I walked through the cypress tree lined entrance to the cemetery. Every month I visited Mom, telling her about my life and how much I loved her. Today I told her about Senator Guidry, knowing she would have been terribly disappointed with me. Even so, she'd have hugged me as tightly as possible…I missed her hugs and kisses.

Arranging the flowers by her headstone, I said my goodbyes and promised to return next month.

Arriving at my office with makeup re-applied and coffee in hand, I knew I would be in for a busy week when I saw the stack of messages on my assistant's desk. My name is Jessie Jane Edwards. Mom called me "JJ". My friends usually call me "Jess".

"Good morning, Lee. Seems we had a few calls over the weekend," I said with a nod at the messages.

"Good morning to you as well. Looks like you're a popular lady," Lee replied with a smile. Lee had worked for me for more than three years, and he was one of the best researchers I've ever known.

"Not sure 'popular' is the right word but thank you anyway. Can you return the calls and get more details please? I want to work more on the Johnston case."

"Sure thing. Since you don't live under a rock, I know you heard about Guidry dying after his trial. What do you think about it?"

A smile creased my face as I thought about Guidry collapsing. "Two things…no make that three things. One, the prick deserved to die. Two, justice was served even if it wasn't by lethal injection, and three, it saved a lot of money because he would've kept wasting taxpayer money on bullshit projects. What about you?"

Lee cocked his head thoughtfully, "I guess the world losing a jackass like that really isn't a terrible thing."

"Perfectly stated," I said, wondering what Lee would think if he ever found out my truth. "After making the calls, please stack the messages and your notes in order of importance on my desk." Lee nodded his understanding.

It was a typical Monday for a private detective. Lots of phone work, tracking down leads and setting up interviews on the cases I was working. My practice is small, with Lee and I as the only employees. The office is on the Northshore of New Orleans in a small town named Mandeville. The best part of being on the fourth floor of the building was being able to look out my window and see Lake Pontchartrain. I discovered years before that watching the waves dancing on the lake was the best way for me to clear my mind. And a clear mind was much better at finding the small missing pieces to help solve cases.

Dad called later in the morning. "Hey Jess, how about lunch today?"

"Thanks, Dad, but I'm meeting Becky for lunch. Does another day work?" I asked.

"Sarah and I are going to the beach Wednesday. Why don't we get together when I get back?"

"Sure thing, have a great time. I love you, Dad," I said before hanging up.

Dad and I have a complicated relationship. He'd remarried too soon after Mom died, and I never quite got past it. Even at 12 years old, I knew he was making a mistake. Sure enough, the marriage lasted less than five years. I'm sure I didn't help the situation; I was hard-headed and didn't care for Wendy. That was not a healthy combination, and my bad behavior affected my relationship with Dad. For a long time, he blamed me for the resulting divorce. Over the years, we were able to work through it and now had a good relationship again. I loved him and he loved me, but it just wasn't the same as how I loved Mom.

I pushed away my memories and went back to the Johnston case. Before I realized it, time had arrived for me to meet my best friend in the world, Becky Jordan. Becky served as FBI Agent Jordan during the day, and my drinking buddy at night. We met every Monday at a little hole-in-the-wall restaurant that serves the best red beans and rice.

Walking in, I saw Becky was already seated. It was hard to miss her long, red hair even when tied up in a bun. She stood and we gave each other a brief hug before sitting.

"How was your weekend on the coast?", I asked knowing Becky and her boyfriend had gone to the Mississippi Gulf Coast for gambling and a concert.

"The concert was great, the gambling not so much," she replied with a big grin. "What did you do with your weekend?"

"Not too much," I replied with a shrug.

At that moment, our waiter approached. He'd served us several times before, so knew us well.

"Good afternoon," Bobby greeted us with a smile.

"Hi Bobby," we replied simultaneously.

"Let me guess, red beans and rice for both of you?" We smiled and nodded affirmatively. "Side salads and teas as well?" Again, we nodded our assent. "Well, aren't you ladies easy!"

I raised an eyebrow, and Becky coughed slightly. Poor Bobby turned beet red, and stammered, "I, uh, I didn't mean it that way."

"Bobby," I started, while giving him my most direct stare. "You should choose your words more carefully. We don't..." and before I could finish my fake lecture, Becky burst out laughing, causing me to break character. "Don't worry, we were just having fun with you!"

Bobby exhaled and smiled, "I really didn't mean it."

"We know, we know. Now off with you!" I pronounced with a wave of my hand. He scooted away as fast as he could, while still trying to retain some measure of dignity. We both laughed at his discomfort before Becky leaned towards me and lowered her voice.

"Can you believe Senator Guidry kicked the bucket like that?"

I shrugged and replied, "Karma's a bitch." Becky chuckled and sat back.

"That may be, but I can't wait to see the autopsy report."

"No need," I replied. "Massive heart attack accompanied by sudden cardiac arrest. The way he dropped like a rock tells me it wasn't just a run of the mill heart attack. With CPR started so quickly, I suspect if it were a simple heart attack, the piece of shit would have lived." I clenched my jaw thinking of the way his wife had been murdered. "He really didn't suffer enough in my opinion."

"That's right, I forgot you were a doctor," Becky said as she nodded her head. "Even though the FBI wasn't directly involved in the investigation, we kept up with it and I'm sure he killed his wife."

"Yep, and the universe came for his ass." Which was true, since I'm part of the universe. As for being a doctor, Becky was right about that also. I'd graduated from Texas A&M's medical school, but never practiced medicine.

"And speaking of my being a doctor, I noticed your thyroid appears to be a bit swollen. You should go and have someone check it out."

Becky ran her fingers across her thyroid. "I can't feel anything."

"Because you're not a doctor. Trust me on this, get it checked out." I paused before continuing, "Changing gears, you going to kickboxing class today?"

"Can't today, but I'm planning on going Tuesday and Thursday."

Our drinks arrived, along with the salads. We dug in and soon our meals were delivered as well. The rest of lunch was spent in casual chatter about things that didn't really matter. As much as I love Becky, I didn't feel like visiting with her too long, so I made my escape right after we finished eating. The weekend had unsettled me more than it should.

Arriving back at the office, I found Lee had completed his task and the messages were neatly stacked on my desk, along with his notes. The message on top was marked urgent and involved a missing child.

I read the notes before picking up the phone to return the call. The phone rang once before being answered, "Hello?"

"Good afternoon. My name is Jessie Edwards from Edwards' Investigations and I'm returning your call."

"Thank you for calling me back. I'm so worried, I don't know what to do," the frantic, high-pitched voice replied.

"I understand. Is this Mrs. Alice Reynolds?"

"Yes, I'm sorry, I should have introduced myself."

"That's quite okay Mrs. Reynolds. How long has your daughter been missing?"

"Please call me Alice, and Madison has been gone for three days now. I called the police and everyone has been out looking, but we don't know what else to do," she sobbed into the phone.

"Alice, I'm happy to help however I can. May I come to your home to speak with you and your husband?"

"Of course, but he's my ex-husband. Dale doesn't live here anymore, but I'll call him to come over. When can you be here?"

I checked her address on the notes and knew the area well. "I can be there in 30 minutes if that works for you."

"The sooner the better," and Alice hung up the phone.

I grabbed my purse, leaving Lee a note telling him I was going to the Reynolds'. Mid-afternoon traffic was relatively light, so I was able to make it a few minutes ahead of time. The house was a run down, older brick home on a large lot. The area was semi-rural with lots of empty land and woods nearby. There were several cars and trucks in the yard, so I parked to the side making sure not to block anyone in.

Ringing the doorbell brought a quick response of running feet and the door being opened by a tall, thin teenage boy. His curly brown hair was hanging partially over his eyes. "Hi, my name is Jessie and your mom is expecting me."

"Yes ma'am. She's in the den over here," he said as he led the way. A short walk down the hallway had me entering a small den. The ceiling was so low I felt like I needed to duck, and I'm only 5'7". Seated on a worn striped couch was a distressed woman with unkempt brown hair, and a heavyset man wearing jeans and a greasy t-shirt. Both stood up as I entered the room.

"Hi, I'm Jessie Edwards." I paused, meeting their eyes. "I'm sorry you're going through this. Let's see what I can do to help."

"Thank you for coming. I'm Alice and this is Dale," she said nodding towards the man with the greasy t-shirt. I stuck my hand out and shook both of their hands. Alice then looked towards the boy who'd answered the door. "This is our son, Michael." He gave me a small wave from across the room.

I nodded to Michael before turning my attention back to the parents. "Alice, how about I tell you what I know so far and you correct any information I have wrong. From there, I'll ask you some questions, so I have a better understanding of everything. Sound good?'

"Of course," Alice said as she and Dale sat back down on the couch. I sat on a nearby chair and pulled out my notes to recite the facts as I understood them.

"Madison is 14 years old, 5'2" and weighs about 100 pounds. She has long brown hair and was last seen in the yard here after school. She was wearing jeans and a yellow concert t-shirt." I paused to look up and both parents were nodding so I continued, "She's in 8ᵗʰ grade at Regional Middle School and makes good grades. My notes from your call with Lee indicate you've been in touch with the police and searches have been conducted in the immediate area with no results. Did they bring dogs in?"

Alice replied, "Yes, but they didn't find anything."

"Do you have a picture of Madison that I can keep?"

Alice reached into her purse and pulled out a school picture. I looked at it carefully and saw a sweet, beautiful child smiling back at me. Down deep I knew if someone hurt her, I would end them in the most painful manner possible.

"Thank you," I said after my review of the picture. "What have the police told you?"

"They've put out an Amber Alert and started speaking with our neighbors and Madison's friends. We don't have any updates though."

"Who is your main point of contact at the police department?" I asked, hoping it was someone I had a good relationship with.

"Detective Arnold is leading the investigation," came the quick reply. That was good news for me as Sam Arnold and I had a good working relationship. He was also my ex-boyfriend, but the parting had been mostly amicable.

"Great! Detective Arnold and I have worked closely together on several cases. He'll help me get up to speed on their work. Once I know where they stand, I'll formulate a plan and review it with you both to make sure you are comfortable with what I'm doing. Are you good with that?"

Both nodded, so I continued, "And now for the part of the conversation that's never easy...we need to discuss my fees." Alice and

Dale quickly broke eye contact, letting me know my fees were not going to be easy for them to handle.

After an uncomfortable pause, Dale finally spoke up. "We, umm, don't have a lot of money, but we can pay you something." Oh boy, looks like I wouldn't be covering my costs with this one.

"My normal rates are $1000 per day, prorated of course, plus expenses. And I usually require a $5000 retainer in order to start a case." The shocked looks on their faces told me that was going to be a problem. "Tell you what," I continued as quickly as I could. "Why don't we waive the retainer to help you out?"

Alice took over at this point. "Is there any wiggle room on your daily fee? We will do everything necessary to find Madison, but we don't have much money." She looked around the house before returning her hopeful gaze to me.

I looked up to the ceiling and considered their plight. It was apparent money was an issue for them, and I couldn't get Madison's face out of my mind. "I can cut my fee in half, but I can't do anything more than that," I finally stated. Both brightened at my offer and Dale stuck his hand out saying, "Deal!"

I took his hand with a firm grip and gave them my best look of determination.

Climbing into my car, I started it and pulled my phone out. Dialing Sam brought back memories of other times I'd called him, though those calls were for more personal reasons. Two rings later, Sam answered.

"Hi Jess, what's up?"

Sam had such a smooth, deep voice that it was almost hypnotic. "Lots going on Sam. I hear you're working the missing girl case." I paused, waiting for a confirmation that didn't come. "The family hired me to help them through the process. Can we get together to review what you've got so far?"

13

Another pause told me Sam was considering what to say. "I'm working the case, but I'm pretty busy. Can we touch base in a day or two when things settle down?"

That wasn't going to work for me at all. "Come on Sam. I won't take much of your time and maybe I'll think of an angle that hasn't been covered." I knew Sam was as dedicated as they come, and if I could offer something that might help, he'd be hard-pressed to pass on it.

"Yeah, okay. Meet me at Rango's Roadhouse at 7pm. You get to buy me dinner." I agreed and drove back to the office to finish the day.

CHAPTER 3

I was still at my desk when I noticed it was almost 7pm. Uttering a curse, I texted Sam informing him I'd be a couple of minutes late. After driving like a madwoman, I made it less than 10 minutes late. Sam was seated in the back corner with a large folder beside him. I grinned, knowing he had come through for me.

Seeing me approach, Sam's 6'2" chiseled ebony frame slid out of the booth and gave me a powerful hug. He looked down on me with a smile on his lips, but sadness in his eyes. "Good to see you, Jess."

"You too, you hunk of gorgeous man," I replied, with my biggest, brightest smile. "Seriously though, I know it wasn't easy for you to get away on short notice. Thank you."

"I'd say 'anything for you', but my girlfriend wouldn't take kindly to that," he said chuckling. A little pain shot through my chest while I half-heartedly laughed with him. We sat on opposite sides of the booth and Sam slid the folder to me. "This is everything we have right now. Take your time, but you can't get copies of anything."

I nodded and started my review. The waitress came by and took our orders. Silence reigned at the table for the next 15 minutes as I read through the file. Interviews of family members, friends and neighbors were all included. Everyone who knew Madison well agreed she wasn't the kind of kid to run off. She didn't have a romantic partner, and everyone was at a loss.

The inspection of the area found so many tire tracks that it was going to be almost impossible to determine if any were from a kidnapper's car. The police were trying to compare the tracks against all known cars that had been there, but it was going to be a long process.

The search of the area had been completed by over 50 people, and with dogs. The dogs trailed multiple scents for Madison, but all ended within 100 yards of the property. So if someone took her, they would have had to pick her up or place her in something to take her away. A nearby pond had been searched by divers with no success.

I didn't want to duplicate any of the work unless I found something unusual, and there was nothing that I could find to cause me to feel like re-interviewing most of the people. I did want to speak with Madison's brother though. I suspected he may have been a little intimidated by the police and may know more than he told them.

I pushed the file back. "Thanks. Looks like your people are doing a very thorough job."

"They are. Everyone takes a case like this to heart."

"I get it. I'll be speaking with a few of the people again and I'll let you know if I develop anything that's not covered here."

Sam nodded, but didn't say anything while the food was being delivered. Between bites, he looked up at me and said, "I know it's been a while since we broke up, but I still miss you."

I saw pain and confusion in his eyes and flashed back to the day I ended the relationship. It was right after I'd terminated a real dirtbag, and I couldn't stop thinking about getting caught some day. And when that day arrived, I kept imagining the depth of betrayal he would feel. I simply couldn't put him through that, but there was no way to really explain it either.

"I'm sorry, Sam. I'm toxic, it's as simple as that. Being around me long-term would be devastating to you and I'm not willing to cause you pain." I saw defeat in his eyes as he heard a message for the second time that I knew he would never understand.

"Back to the case," I said looking for a redirection. "Have you pulled a list of registered sex offenders within a 10- or 20-mile radius?"

He grunted slightly before replying, "It's been requested, but with all the moving parts, we haven't been quick about getting through the list," he said shaking his head.

"Only so much time in a day so don't beat yourself up. What about social media?"

He nodded, "Yes, we have access to her accounts. They're being reviewed now."

"Please let me know if you find anything there."

As I was talking, Sam pulled out his phone and sent a quick text. I didn't ask what it was about, not wanting to know if it was to his girlfriend.

The meal ended with an awkward hug and good-bye, and with mutual assurances we would update the other on any progress. The next day was going to be a long one for me so I went home, took a hot bath and climbed in bed for a restless night of sleep.

I woke up the next morning remembering one dream vividly. In it, Senator Guidry had been screaming at me. He was pointing and yelled repeatedly at me, "You don't have the right! You don't have the right!" He was probably correct, but he shouldn't have slaughtered his wife.

My first task was to meet with the Reynolds and give them my game plan. I called to set an appointment for 10am and asked their son to be available if possible. They told me he was home, having not gone to school that day. After arriving and exchanging pleasantries, I cut to the chase.

"I spoke with Detective Arnold and reviewed their information. They are doing an excellent job of being thorough in their investigation.

No new leads have come up, but I did suggest to them they get a list of all people on the sex offenders' registry in the area. Once compiled, the police will interview each of them starting with the ones closest to your home."

"Do you think it could be one of those perverts?" Alice asked.

"We never know, but it's a good idea to cover all possibilities as quickly as possible." I saw them shudder thinking about the consequences of their daughter being in the hands of a sex offender. "With your permission, I'd like to go over my plan of action."

Both agreed so I pulled a binder out of my briefcase. "First, I would like to speak with your son. I know he was interviewed already, but I want to make sure we get every possible angle covered. After that, I'd like to search through Madison's room and the house to see if the police may have missed something. Next, I want to go through Madison's list of friends with you to make sure the police have all the names."

I looked at each parent and asked, "Good so far?" When they nodded, I continued, "Fourth, I didn't see anything with regards to adults Madison has regular contact with. Music teachers, coaches, anyone like that. I'd like to develop that list and start speaking with each of them. Any of these could possibly lead me to another avenue, so I will be flexible in the approach. And finally, I have a few more questions for you. Is it okay for me to ask you the questions now?"

Alice and Dale looked at each other before turning to me and nodding. "These questions may be uncomfortable, and I mean no disrespect, but I must ask them." I didn't wait for a response before beginning my interrogation.

"Do you know if Madison was sexually active?" Alice blanched a bit before shaking her head and answering, "I don't think so."

"Had Madison asked about getting on the pill?" Alice again shook her head.

"Either of you have a serious fight with Madison within the last two weeks?" Alice shook her head, but Dale nodded slowly. "Well, Madison wanted to go out with one of the black boys from school, and I told her no. We got to yelling at each other so much that she came back to her mother's and didn't stay with me like she usually does."

Oh great, another racist idiot I thought while keeping a straight face. "Who was the boy, and is his name on the list of friends you gave to the police?"

"I don't know his name, I never asked," came the quiet reply. I turned to Alice, "Do you know who this boy is?" She nodded and answered, "Reggie. He's in her class at school."

"Good information," I said writing down the details. "Next question, do either of you believe Madison has been taking drugs, either illegal or prescription pills that aren't hers?

Both shook their heads immediately. "What about drinking? Does Madison drink with her friends?"

Alice nodded, "I caught her drinking beer with a couple of friends one day when I came home early." I raised my eyebrows, looking for her to continue. "She was pretty embarrassed and went on and on about how it was the first time...total bullshit for sure. I could tell she was lying."

I cut in, "Was she taking your beer or getting it somewhere else?"

"I don't drink beer, and since Dale's been gone, we don't keep any in the house," came the reply.

"Interesting...someone has to be buying beer for her," I said, almost to myself. I added this tidbit to my notes so I would remember to ask Michael what he knew about this. If there were an older person involved without the parents knowing, they were a person of interest in my opinion. I looked through my notes before concluding, "I know you gave access to the police to Madison's social media accounts. I will need them as well." Both nodded as I continued. "Can I speak with Michael please? And we need to be alone. He may tell me things he wouldn't be comfortable saying in front of you."

"Of course," Alice replied. "I'll go get him."

While we waited for Michael to come in, I looked Dale over. It was obvious he was uncomfortable, and I wondered if it was because of the awful situation or if he knew something more. Before I could pry, Michael entered with Alice.

"As I was saying Michael, Ms. Edwards wants to speak with you alone. Please answer her questions as best you can," Alice said as they walked to me. Michael nodded his understanding, and the parents left the room. I motioned to the couch saying, "Hello again Michael. I know we met before, but I'm sure you've seen a lot of people since then. I'm Jessie, and your parents asked me to help find Madison. Please think carefully while answering my questions. Any little detail could be important so tell me everything, even if you don't think it matters. Do you understand?"

He nodded, so I continued, "Do you have any questions before we start?"

He shook his head, prompting me to begin the questioning. "Did you know Madison drinks with her friends?"

Michael's head was down as he leaned forward, elbows on knees. "Yes."

"Do you drink with them too?"

Again, a quiet answer, "Sometimes."

"How old are you?"

"17."

"Where do y'all get the beer?" I watched him carefully to see if I could pick anything up from his body language.

"Here and there."

"Come on, you can do better than that. Does one of your friends usually bring it, or is it just whoever can get it?"

"I don't want to get anyone in trouble," Michael said.

"Look at me Michael," I said firmly. He raised his eyes, while barely lifting his head. I continued, "You need to understand this, I'm here to find your sister. The only person who's going to get in trouble is any person involved with Madison's disappearance. But if you don't give me all the information you have, you may be keeping me from helping Madison, and that's not cool. So please answer me truthfully. None of this is going back to your mom and dad."

"My friend's older brother buys for us," he finally confessed.

"What's your friend's name and what's his older brother's name?"

"My friend is Tommy Bordelon, and his brother is Gary."

"How old is Gary?"

"Like 22 or 23."

We were on a roll, and I wanted to keep the questions coming fast and furious. "Where does Gary live?"

"Somewhere in Abita Springs, but I don't know where."

"Where were you the day Madison disappeared?" I'd learned that changing topics quickly can be an effective tool when questioning hesitant witnesses. Michael paused, digesting the change in direction.

"I was home."

"I know the police asked you a lot of questions, and I may repeat some of them, but please tell me everything you can about what happened."

He nodded, "I got home from school around 3pm. Madison was already home since her school gets out a little earlier than mine. She was out in the yard playing with the dog when the bus dropped me off. I didn't really talk to her, I just went inside and put my backpack in my room and went to the kitchen to make a sandwich."

"Where was your mom?"

"She was still at work. She usually doesn't get home until 5:30pm or so."

"You made your sandwich, then what?"

"I turned on the tv, sat on the couch watching it and eating my sandwich."

"What were you watching?"

"The business channel. I like to see what the market did each day when I get home." He must have seen a surprised look on my face before continuing somewhat sheepishly, "I want to be a trader someday."

Shame on me for pre-judging people the way I did when I met Michael. "That's a wonderful and challenging career. I hope you get there," I said trying to cover for my mistake.

"Thanks," he mumbled.

"Did Madison come inside at all before you noticed she was gone?"

"No, the only time I saw her again was when I heard the dog barking, so I looked out the window. My friend Tommy's truck was stopped in the street and Madison was talking to him. I figured they were setting up the next beer run."

I hadn't remembered anything about this in the paperwork, so I asked, "Did you tell the police about this?"

"I don't remember. They asked me a bunch of questions like you are, but I'm not sure if they asked that." I made a mental note to call Sam.

"What kind of truck does Tommy drive?"

"Black Toyota Tacoma."

"What's Tommy's last name again?"

"Bordelon."

"Do you know about what time it was when you looked outside?"

"3:40pm," he said with conviction.

"That's very specific, how do you remember the time?"

The network always cuts to commercial at 3:40pm so that was a good time for me to see why the dog was barking. That was the last time I saw her."

"When did you start to wonder about her?"

"Right after the show ended at 4pm, the dog was whining at the door, so I let him in. Madison wasn't with the dog, so that's when I started wondering what was going on. I figured she must have gone to a friend's house so didn't really think much about it right then."

I shifted topics again. "Does Madison have a boyfriend or girlfriend that your parents don't know about?"

"Not really. I don't think she's into anyone right now."

"What about before? Was there anyone she was 'into'?"

He nodded, "She was crushing on a kid named Percy, but I don't think they ever got together."

"Percy in her grade at school?"

"Yeah."

My phone chirped as I was making a note. It was Sam's number, so I told Michael that was all for the time being and stepped out to answer. "Hi, Sam. Got any good news?"

"We may have a hit on a sex offender. There's a 31-year-old male who lives two miles from the Reynolds' house. He served ten years for sexual assault on a minor and has been out for the past two years. One of our guys stopped by to question him, and the ex-con freaked out. I know that's not conclusive, but it's a start."

"Are you getting a search warrant?"

"Yeah, but 'freaking out' is a little weak for most judges so we're running into delays."

"I can see that presents a problem. I'm at the Reynolds' right now so give me the name and address. I'll swing by and visit with the gent."

"You don't have any official authorization, understood?" Lee stated emphatically. It was cute how he thought he was playing me.

"Understood boss, now give me the details," He recited the information and admonished me to be careful. Of course, he didn't know how well and easily I could defend myself, but the thought was appreciated.

Five minutes later, I was sitting in my idling car looking at a rundown trailer placed in the middle of a trash strewn, overgrown yard. Snakes were the thing I needed to fear most, and lord, I really hate snakes.

I had to be careful on how I played the suspect, a Mr. Darryl Picou. I decided to use my charm and feminine wiles to get inside his trailer. I unbuttoned the top button of my blouse, feeling cheap and dirty as I did it. I'd do anything for that little girl though, and a smile, a laugh and a little cleavage can go a long way with a scumbag like Darryl. Walking carefully through the shortest grass I could find got me to the front door. My knock was rewarded by footsteps and a gruff, "Who's there?"

"Mr. Picou? My name is Jessie and I'm hoping you can help me out," I said, trying to sound as sweet and innocent as possible.

"What do you need?" came the clipped reply.

"Can you please open the door so we can speak face-to-face?"

The door cracked open and his unshaven, lean face peered out. "How'd you know my name?"

Shit, good question. "It's on your mailbox." At least I hoped it was.

"Oh...what do you want?"

The moment of truth had arrived. I stepped a little to the side to give him a better look at me and said, "I just need a moment of your time. I'm trying to help some friends of mine with a problem.

He looked me up and down carefully, but surprisingly, not in a leering way. "You a cop?"

I smiled and shook my head. "No, just a friend of the Reynolds from down the road."

He didn't say anything, but he pushed the door open wider and walked back into the trailer. I did as well and was immediately assaulted by disgusting smells. He motioned me to sit, but there was no way I was going on his filthy couch. "Thanks, but I'm fine standing."

He sat and grabbed a beer can off the table. "What do you need?" I had quickly scanned the small area when I walked in, but hadn't seen anything of interest other than a crack pipe. I decided to level with him to see his reaction.

"You've heard about the missing girl?"

He gave no reaction, other than saying, "Yeah, it's all over the news."

"With you living so close, I was hoping you may have heard or seen something. Madison is only 14 years old and we need to bring her back to her family." I doubted sympathy would work, but I wasn't leaving anything in my pocket on this one.

"Can't help you," was all he said.

"Maybe you've heard someone talking, or seen a suspicious vehicle around?"

"Nope."

"Do you have any friends that you can ask to see if they heard anything?"

"Nope."

This wasn't going well, but he hadn't kicked me out yet. I also knew I wouldn't get anywhere asking if I could look around. I rubbed my hands on my forehead thinking of what to do next when he spoke.

"Have you talked to people at the homeless camp?"

I looked at him thoughtfully. This either was a really good misdirection play on his part, or he was trying to come up with something to help. My gut told me he was on the level.

"No, but that's a good idea." I thanked him for his time and gave him my card before leaving. Safely back through the snake pit, I called Sam who answered immediately.

"How'd it go?" he asked without a greeting.

"Not too bad. I got inside, but don't think Madison is there. Nothing he said or did leads me to believe he's covering up. The reason he freaked about your guy showing up is he's an ex-con with a crack pipe. I'm pretty sure he's not involved in our problem."

"If we get the warrant, we'll check it out anyway. Anything else?"

"Yeah, Picou asked if I'd spoken to anyone at the homeless encampment that's close to the house. Have you guys canvassed there?"

"We did, but most of the people scattered when they saw our team, so we didn't get to speak to many of them."

"Okay, I'll swing by there and see what I can find out. I'll let you know what I hear."

"Thanks, Jess," which was quickly followed by a click.

CHAPTER 4

The homeless encampment was in a small patch of woods near the intersection of a highway and the interstate. I suspect only 10-15 people called the area home, with tents scattered around the woods. It was close to a convenience store and a couple of fast food joints. It was also only a mile from the Reynolds' house.

At first glance, I didn't see anyone in the area. I walked into the woods a short way and came upon a middle-aged, dangerously gaunt man whose grey hair was so thinning it looked like he suffered from radiation poisoning. He calmly regarded me as I approached. Not wanting to scare him off, I stopped well short of him.

"Good afternoon, my name is Jessie Edwards and I'm looking for a lost girl." I hoped this would prompt a response but was disappointed when he didn't react at all. "Is there any chance you or one of your friends here has seen a 14-year-old girl wandering around?" I had the picture of Madison in my outstretched hand. He walked closer to look.

He took the picture carefully from me, holding it close to his face. After a moment, he said, "I've seen her."

I froze, unable to believe I hit pay dirt so fast. Excitedly I asked, "Do you remember when and where?"

"I may be homeless, but I'm not stupid. Of course I remember. I saw her at the convenience store a couple of days ago."

"May I have your name?" He looked at me warily, so I quickly added, "I just want to know how to address you."

You can call me Slim.

"Thanks, Slim. This girl is Madison Reynolds. She's been missing for four days now. Do you recall what day you saw her?"

"Is today Tuesday?"

"Yes."

"Then it was Friday when I saw her," he stated without hesitation.

"That's the day she went missing. What you're telling me could be really important so please try to remember everything."

He nodded as he said, "What do you want to know?"

"About what time was it when you saw her?"

"Around 5 o'clock I'd say."

"Do you know for sure?"

"I didn't look at a clock, but I go to the store every day around that time to get something to eat and use the bathroom."

"Where was she exactly when you saw her and how is it that you remember her?"

He absently scratched his jaw as he replied, "She was inside with a guy getting beer. I remember her 'cause she gave me some money out of her pocket. It surprised me with her being so young."

"Can you describe the guy she was with?"

"Big guy, older than her but still young. Black hair," he paused as he thought. "Can't really remember anything else about him."

"Did you hear them talking?"

"Don't remember hearing anything."

"Did you happen to see what kind of car they were driving?" I was having trouble containing my excitement, knowing this was the first solid lead on the case.

"Yeah, when I came out of the store, they were sitting in a black pickup."

"What kind of pickup?"

"I don't remember."

"What happened then?"

"Nothing. I walked away and that was that."

"And you haven't seen her again, right?"

"Right," he confirmed.

I reached in my purse and grabbed a $100 bill. "I don't want to offend you, but could you use some extra help?" I extended my hand.

Slim looked down with a sad smile, "Generosity is always appreciated ma'am." I smiled back and gave him a hug. When I broke the hug, I asked, "Are you on Medicare or Medicaid?"

He nodded, "Yes, they tried treating me for cancer, but it didn't work. Why?"

"I happen to be a doctor also, and it did appear to me that you have cancer. Do you know anything about hospice care?"

"A little, I guess. That's when they take care of you right before you die, right?"

"It doesn't have to be right before you die, but that's how it's used most often. You may want to ask about it before the pain becomes too bad. They really can help you be more comfortable."

"I'll pass, but thanks for caring," he said, giving me the same sad smile. I gave him my card and told him to call me if he ever needed anything. It was apparent to me Slim didn't have much time left.

I called Sam immediately upon my return to the car. His phone went straight to voicemail. "Sam, it's Jess. Call me immediately!" I almost screamed into the phone. Not only did I need to speak with Sam, I needed more time with Michael. I gunned the engine and went back to the house.

Michael answered the door when I knocked. "Hi Ms. Edwards," he greeted me.

"Hi Michael. I need to ask you a few more questions about your friend, Tommy." I didn't wait for his acknowledgement. "Can you describe how Tommy looks?"

Michael had a curious look on his face as he replied, "He's about my height, so that'd be 5'10" or so. He's a little heavy. Has light brown hair."

That description didn't match up well with Slim's description of the guy, so I changed direction. "Can you call Tommy please? Put him on speaker and tell him I'm trying to help your family find Madison."

He nodded, pulled out his phone and hit the call button. The speaker was activated so I heard when Tommy answered. "What's up bro?"

Michael handled it beautifully. "Hey Tommy, I need your help. My family hired a private investigator to help us find Madison. She's right here and I need you to answer her. Big favor to me, k?"

"Sure man, anything for you." I jumped in at this point. "Hi Tommy. My name is Jessie Edwards and I'm hoping you can answer some questions. Last Friday, when Madison disappeared, did you drive by Michael's house and talk with Madison around 4 o'clock?"

There was only a short pause, "No ma'am." I saw Michael's face twist in surprise and before I could follow up the question, he jumped in.

"I saw you! I saw you in the road talking to Madison!" And of course this was the moment Sam called me back. *Shit!* I had to send him to voicemail.

Tommy fired right back. "Bullshit dude, I was at my house doing yardwork." Michael's face was getting redder and redder; it was obvious he was about to blow his lid, so I jumped in.

"Tommy? Any chance someone borrowed your truck?"

"My brother may have. He's got a key to it."

"What does your brother look like?"

"He's a big dude, like over 6' tall and probably 230 pounds and has short black hair." And all the pieces fell into place.

"Thanks for your help Tommy. I know Michael appreciates it too." I didn't wait for his response before hanging up. Turning to Michael, I said, "That was really important. I hope you and Tommy cool off and don't lose your friendship." It was clear he had settled down when he replied, "Nah, we'll be good."

I stepped outside and rang Sam back. He answered immediately, "What've you got?"

"Big news my friend. I've got a witness who places Madison at the convenience store on Hwy 21 around 5pm Friday. The witness says she was with a guy buying beer and described the guy as big with black hair. They were in a black pickup, make unknown. We need the surveillance tapes from that store bad Sam."

"I'm on it. Who's the witness?"

"One of the homeless guys, goes by the name 'Slim'. Madison gave him some money and he remembered her because of it."

"Fantastic, great job, Jess!"

"Don't thank me yet, because there's more," I teased.

His voice turned professional again, "Out with it then. We need this, Jess."

"Madison's brother, Michael, saw Madison speaking with someone who was driving his friend Tommy Bordelon's truck. Michael thought it was Tommy, but I just spoke with Tommy and he claims to have been home working in the yard. He says his brother, Gary, has the keys to his truck and may have borrowed it. And the kicker is, Gary meets the description of the guy buying beer with Madison."

"Outstanding! We'll get the video from the convenience store and

I'll send one of my guys to visit with Gary. You don't happen to have his address, do you?"

"No, all I know is he lives in Abita Springs." We ended the call, again agreeing to keep each other informed. I knocked on the door so I could update Alice. She let me in, and I suggested we speak privately. Michael went back to his room.

"We had a big breakthrough today, Alice. I found a witness who placed Madison at the convenience store down the road around 5pm on Friday. The police are going there now to get the surveillance tapes. Do you know Tommy's brother, Gary Bordelon?"

"Not really. I know Tommy very well and I've seen his brother, but don't know him. Why?"

"Gary may have borrowed Tommy's truck and stopped by the house. We just want to cover all the bases." I continued my line of questioning, "Is it possible Madison has a crush on Gary, or they're having some sort of relationship?"

Alice shrugged, "I guess anything's possible." I could tell she was thinking of her 14-year-old daughter having a relationship with a 22-year-old man, and it was a most disturbing thought.

CHAPTER 5

With nothing else to do for Madison, I returned to the office to work on other files. It was late in the day when my phone chirped, Sam calling with hopefully some good news.

"Hi, Sam. What's the update?"

"We ran Gary through the system and got his address, license, car details and criminal record. Any of that interest you?"

"All of it. He has his own car?"

"Yeah, it's a 2011 red Camero, plate 279-WDC." I wrote down the information as I asked, "Got a picture of him from the license?"

"I'll email it to you."

"What about his address?" To which he recited the address.

"Any criminal record?"

"Only drunk and disorderly a couple years ago."

"Was he at the apartment when your team arrived?"

"Nobody answered the door, and we don't have a warrant yet. We pulled the video from the convenience store though, and it shows them together right at 5pm like the witness says. The truck was a black Toyota, but we didn't get a good shot of the license."

I cut him off. "That's his brother Michael's truck. I can get the plate number for you if you need it."

"No need, I can pull it from DMV, but thanks anyway."

I was thinking of what I would do next, but wanted to see if Sam had other ideas. "What's next?" I asked.

"We're getting a warrant now. Should be back to the apartment within the hour I imagine. I also put the Camaro out on the wire state-wide. Maybe one of the good guys will spot him."

I could feel the noose tightening and wondered if Gary even knew he and Madison were being looked for so aggressively. I had to imagine even a dumbass would realize the cops would be searching for a missing teenage girl. I just prayed Madison was still alive and well. "One last thing Sam, did anyone speak to Gary's family to ask about his whereabouts?"

"Beat you to it. We spoke with them less than thirty minutes ago. They haven't seen him in days."

"Guess it was too much to hope for."

We ended the conversation and I called Alice with the update. I didn't want to either get her hopes up or worry her even more, so I tried to stick to the facts. She took the information as well as possible. I assured her she would get updates from me just as soon as I heard anything.

With nothing left to do, and too much unspent energy burning through me, I went to kickboxing to take my frustration out on anyone who dared to spar with me. It was quite satisfying feeling feet and fists sink into my opponent. Even getting hit felt good, anything to get my mind off the situation.

I was in the dressing room when Sam called back. "Yes?" I answered.

"Gary wasn't at the apartment, but we did find a girl's shoe. Detective Tullier is going to the Reynold's right now to see if they recognize it."

"Oh shit," was all I could say. "Any luck with the neighbors?"

"None at all." We disconnected and I immediately called Alice. She answered on the second ring.

"Hello?"

"Hi Alice, it's Jess. The police found a woman's shoe at Gary's apartment. Nobody was home so they are bringing it to you to see if it's Madison's."

A small, but audible gasp could be heard. I rushed to calm her down. "A lost shoe doesn't mean anything, so don't read too much into it. It's probably another woman's shoe. And if it is Madison's, it could easily be she misplaced it, and they went to get her new shoes before going somewhere else," I said, knowing how weak it sounded.

"Sure, yeah, sure. Thanks Jess," and Alice hung up. I sat on a bench and repeatedly ran the facts of the case through my head, looking for anything I may have missed. I came up empty each time. Frustration finally drove me off the bench.

I showered, dressed and started the car. Looking at my phone, I saw a text from Sam. It was short and to the point, "Shoe NOT Madison's." I was so relieved, I broke down and cried like a baby, glad to be in a dark parking lot and alone in my car.

Many minutes and even more tears later, I was able to start the drive home. Helplessness flooded through me since finding Gary was out of my control. Right before turning on my street, I decided to forego the comfort of my bed in order to drive around to look for a red Camero. It ended up being a waste of time and gas, but I felt better having made the effort. It was after 1am before I gave up the search. My bed and bad dreams called, so I answered the call and fell into a restless sleep.

The phone woke me at 7:00am. Exhaustedly, I answered without looking at the caller ID, "Hello."

"Rise and shine sleepyhead!" came Becky's way too enthusiastic voice.

"Ugh," was all she got in return.

"Did you go drinking without me last night? I'm going to be pissed if you did," she said playfully.

No, I was up most of the night looking for a missing girl!" I replied, much too sharply. I immediately knew Becky didn't deserve that. "I'm sorry, I'm exhausted and worried, and I've not been sleeping well."

Becky's voice softened. "It's okay honey, I love you anyway."

"Thanks," I said with a little smile crossing my face. "I love you too. What were you calling about?"

"Oh, right. I was calling to see if you're going to class tonight. I was going to skip but changed my plans and will be going."

"You know, that's a good idea. I went last night, and it did help me burn off some energy. But I warn you, don't spar with me unless you want to get your ass handed to you," I laughed as I completed my warning.

"Sure she-devil, you know I'll kick your butt."

"Game on, and the loser buys drinks."

"Perfect. See you at 7," Becky said, signing off. Sparring and a few cocktails were just what I needed. It brightened my mood thinking about chilling with Becky. I made some coffee and went about the morning routine. On the way to the office, I called Sam. He confirmed nothing new had developed overnight, and assured me all hands were on deck trying to find Madison and Gary.

I spent the rest of the day working files with half my brain...the other half being worried about Madison. Late in the day, I called Alice to touch base and let her know nothing new had come up. We chatted for a few minutes, long enough for me to tell the strain was about to break her apart.

Skipping dinner, I went straight to the club for fight night. We geared up, did some calisthenics, and moved into position to spar. Becky bounced up and down on her toes, feinting an occasional jab. I stayed in my defensive position and looked for an opening. A few flurries in, Becky made a mistake and dropped her guard to throw a punch. I sidestepped and threw a right hook which landed on the side of her face. I'd put plenty of power in the punch and it connected with a sold 'thud'. It rocked her back, but didn't knock her down.

"You take a good punch little girl," I teased.

She grimaced, rubbing her cheek. "Yeah, now it's your turn to eat some leather." With that, she unleashed a torrent of kicks and punches. I was able to block or avoid most of them, though she did land a few good shots.

Having withstood her furious assault, I front kicked her to the stomach, knocking her back and leapt to my own attack. Several kick/punch combinations later, Becky stepped back and threw up her hands. "I surrender!" she exclaimed loudly.

I lowered my hands, giving her a big hug. "Let's find other partners to whip up on," to which she eagerly agreed. The rest of the class was spent beating and getting beaten. Once again helping me relieve my stress.

Freshly showered, Becky and I met at a local pub for drinks and appetizers. The waitress seated us and asked for our orders.

"Water and an Old Fashioned," I replied. Becky went with beer. When the waitress left, Becky looked at me seriously and asked, "Are you okay?"

I furrowed my brow a bit and replied, "Sure, I guess. Why?"

"You beat the shit out of me earlier, that's why."

"I'm sorry about that. I let my aggression get out of hand," I acknowledged. "But that means you're buying drinks, right?" I said, trying to lighten the mood.

"You got it, but answer me truthfully. What's wrong?"

I leaned back in my chair. Thoughts of me killing pieces of shit ran through my mind. Even though Becky was absolutely my best friend, I could never tell her what I do. And that sucked.

I went with the obvious answer to cover the bigger problem, "Madison, that's what's got me on edge. We found out she was with an older guy and they've disappeared. I have this terrible fear that he's killed her, even though there's nothing in his past to indicate he's a murderer. Every day that goes by, Madison's family suffers more and more, and I can't do shit about it," I paused before adding weakly, "It's eating me up."

Becky's gaze softened, "I'm sorry honey. I wish I could help you."

I chuckled, "You did…you let me kick your ass." We both laughed and the tension began to drain away. Several drinks later Becky dropped some truth on me.

She looked at me seriously and said, "I finally figured it out."

Having solved the world's problems during previous drinking sessions, I was curious as to what she had figured out. "And that is…?"

She leaned forward conspiratorially and whispered, "You need to get laid."

I busted out laughing, and mid-laugh, I realized *Oh shit, she's right.*

She followed up, "How long's it been? Two years? More?"

"Sam was my last, so yeah, over two years."

As I confirmed everything she was thinking, she leaned back and loudly declared, "Well, there you go! Two years is bullshit for a woman in her prime."

"I'm not dating anyone," I protested.

"So, get on fucking Tinder and find a hot guy. As gorgeous as you are, you'll have the pick of the litter."

"The pick of a bunch of creeps, nice," I said, both disgusted and intrigued. Maybe a little sex could be a good distraction. 'No strings attached' would work given my side business.

"Girl, Tinder isn't as bad as all that. Respectable people are using it now, too. Just find one of them." Finishing my cocktail, I waved the waitress over and dismissed the thought.

I threw caution to the wind and got shit faced, knowing Uber would get me home safely. During the binge, I remembered Becky's thyroid. "Have you scheduled an appointment to have your thyroid checked?"

"Not yet. I figure I'll discuss it with my primary care doctor in a few months," she replied without much thought. It was my turn to get serious.

"I'm not fucking around Becky. It's quite likely you have thyroid cancer and waiting to see a doctor is a terrible idea. If it is cancer, catching it early can mean a world of difference." I stared as forcefully as possible at her during the dressing down.

"Wow, okay. No need to get all Rambo on me," she said defensively.

My tone softened, but my intensity did not. "I don't want to come across like a bitch, but I'm certain you have a serious issue that needs to be looked after." I moved to her side of the table, draping my arm over her shoulder before continuing, "You're my best friend. I love you like a sister and I'm not willing to risk you to a stupid cancer that's easily treated if caught early."

She leaned into me and sighed, "You're right. I'll make the call tomorrow morning." I smiled and hugged her tightly before ordering another round of drinks.

Eventually we wobbled our way out of the bar, and Becky put her arm around my waist. I thought it was for support, but it was her turn to express concern. "Jess, have you considered seeing a professional, like a psychologist? It's obvious how much of a toll your work is taking, and I think you should get some help."

I'd considered it in the past, but once again, how can I possibly tell someone what I do? Nonetheless, she had a good suggestion. "I've thought about it but haven't made the call. You may be right though, it's probably time I spoke with someone."

She smiled and hugged me, "Good 'cause I don't like getting beat up." We were both laughing about that when the Uber pulled up.

Hours later with the bed spinning, I decided drinking so much wasn't such a good idea. It was going to be a long night again, but for a different reason this time.

CHAPTER 6

The phone thankfully didn't wake me. It was my bladder that stepped up to remind me I needed to get out of bed. A quick glance told me it was already 9am, and man, did my head hurt. A lot of water, coffee and some aspirin helped bring the headache to a dull roar. I was in the office for 10:30.

Lee looked me over and just shook his head.

"Hey, don't be judging me," I laughed. He smiled and handed me more messages. Before reaching my desk, Sam called. "We got a hit on the Camaro up in Washington Parish, but the officer lost sight of him before he could turn around. We've got several cars on the way to start canvassing."

I thanked Sam and disconnected. If he was running, it's a pretty good place to hide. It wasn't far away, but it's a very rural area. I decided I may need to consider paying a visit to Gary's brother after school to ask about their contacts in Washington Parish.

In the meantime, it was possible Michael knew a reason why Gary would be there. I told Lee where I was going, and wasted no time getting to the Reynold's house.

As usual, Michael answered the door. "Hi Ms. Edwards. Any luck so far?"

"Maybe, but not sure yet. Do you have any idea what Gary might be doing up in Washington Parish? Does he have some friends there?"

Michael shook his head slightly. "I don't know about that, but he does lease some hunting land there."

My eyebrows rose, "Do you know where?" I asked, my breathing stopped by the revelation.

"Not really, I haven't been there. All I know is it's off Hwy 10 outside Franklinton."

"Do you know who he leases it from?"

"No idea at all," Michael again shook his head.

"Do you know anything about it, like how many acres or does he have a camp on it?"

"He's got a small shack for sure, but I don't know how many acres he has."

I thanked Michael and scrambled for the car. My first call was to Lee, asking him to research Washington Parish utilities for any property with Gary on the account. My next call was to Sam. I got his voicemail, so I left a message about what I had learned. I told him I was going up there to have a look around.

The drive to Franklinton is less than an hour, and I used the time to plan my approach. It was apparent to me I shouldn't be kicking in any doors. But if I could locate the shack and look around, I may find something to help the investigation.

Halfway to Franklinton, Lee called me. "Hi Jess, I found an electric account for Gary." He gave me the address before adding, "There's no phone number attached to the account."

"That's great news. The phone number's no big deal. I'm sure the police have been all over that. I'll let you know what I find when I get there."

Lee's voice expressed his concern as much as his words did. "Be careful, no hero shit. Okay?"

"Thanks, my friend. I promise to be a good girl." I was playing down his concerns, but I appreciated them nonetheless. Googling the address, I saw it was only 20 miles away.

Unlike much of Louisiana which is flat as a parking lot, Washington Parish has some beautiful rolling hills, and it was in this country where Gary had his camp. Google took me straight to the area, but there was no mailbox or sign indicating an address. There was a small dirt road that turned off the highway, disappearing into the woods. A pipe gate was closed and locked to keep out cars.

Before stopping, I drove another mile to make sure I had a good lay of the land. I saw nothing that concerned me, so I turned around and stopped close to the driveway. There was a wide shoulder on the road so I could park without fear of causing an accident. I turned on my flashers, locked the car and started walking. I was just over a rise to the west of the camp, making for an easy hike. If Gary drove in from Franklinton, he wouldn't be able to see my car at all.

Sam chose this moment to return my call. "Hey Sam," I answered.

"Going rogue on me Jess?"

"Not at all. Lee found an electric account in Gary's name so I'm just going past it to see what it looks like," I replied as innocently as possible.

"Don't fuck this up. Where are you and what's the address? I've got guys in the area that can be there in 15 minutes."

"I'm right outside the gate. It's locked and you don't have a warrant to search this property, so back off." I was getting a little agitated at this point. I continued, "If your black and whites show up, and Gary sees them while he's driving here, he'll be in the wind again."

Silence met my arguments, so I wrapped up my thoughts with, "I'm not going to enter the camp. I'm just going to get some intel for you. And I may be able to provide probable cause for you to bust the door down."

Sam hated when I was right, "Just be careful. Call me the moment you see anything."

I disconnected, climbed over a fence and started my trek, all the while staying parallel to the dirt driveway. Less than 5 minutes brought me to a rundown shack. There were no vehicles present, but there were tire tracks everywhere. Some appeared to be fresh based on the way the mud was still damp.

Staying in the woods, I walked a complete circle around the camp, not seeing anything of importance. I finally approached the camp from the back and peered through a dusty window. It was pretty dark inside, therefore it was hard to make much out. It appeared to be a one room camp. I could see a small bed in one corner and a kitchenette on the other side. There was a closed door near to the bed. I figured it was probably the bathroom.

I didn't see Gary or Madison, nor did I see anything identifiable that looked out of place. I snapped some pictures on my phone, both inside through the window and around the outside of the camp. I walked back to the front and took a few pictures of the tire tracks as well, using my foot to help provide scale. With nothing else to do, I hiked back to the car, making sure to stay out of sight of the driveway.

Once seated again in the air conditioning, I called Sam with my report. He said they were already getting a search warrant and had a plain-clothes cop on the way to have a "breakdown" close enough to the driveway that he could watch for Gary. With my job done, I went back to the office.

The excursion had taken up much of the day. That was fine by me since my head wasn't anywhere but on Madison. I locked the office and left at 5pm. My phone rang while I was walking down the stairs. It was Sam again.

"What did you find?" were my first words.

"Madison was likely there. We found some hair on the pillow and blood on the sheets. If I had to guess, they had sex and she was a virgin."

"Anything to indicate if it was consensual or not?"

"We didn't find any ropes, handcuffs or the like, if that's what you mean," he replied. "Other than that, we don't have much. We'll have someone outside the place 24-7 in case they come back."

My mind was working overtime, "What about prints?"

"We dusted everything and have multiple sets. We already have Gary's on file from his previous arrest, but don't have Madison's prints yet. A car was dispatched to the Reynold's house to see if we can find a matching set there."

"Good idea. I'll call Alice to give her a heads up. I'm not going to tell her about the sheets though. No need to upset her," I added.

"Of course, anything else you want to know?"

"Are you going to bring dogs out there to search the area?"

"Considered it, but I don't think we have enough to warrant it yet," he replied. I disagreed and told him so. I pointed out all the reasons to do so, and he countered with having a big presence there could scare off Gary, especially given that it seemed like Madison was a willing partner. I disagreed with his assessment of "willing" but didn't have any evidence to support me. I did tell him that her being a minor, and at a bare minimum statutorily raped, seemed like enough to bring in the dogs. I didn't win the argument, so I ended the call.

I called Alice as the police were pulling up in her yard. I gave her the basics, letting her know the fingerprints would help to confirm if Madison was traveling with Gary. She agreed to be as helpful as possible and thanked me for my assistance.

I replied, "My pleasure. We'll find her soon; I feel it in my bones." And I did feel it. There was no doubt in my mind that Gary had less than 24 hours of freedom left.

Friday arrived with me up and out early. I was in the office before 8am, digging through a file that needed attention. After making some notes for Lee to research, I brought myself back to Madison's case

I was sure Gary had to have another place to go, and it was likely an acquaintance with a place to keep the Camaro unseen. With so much rural land in Washington Parish, it wouldn't be hard to hide a car. I picked up the phone and called Sam.

"Hi Jess," he answered right away.

"Good morning," I replied. "I've been thinking about Gary disappearing. He must have some connection in Washington Parish where he is stashing his car. Have you asked his parents about any friends Gary may have up there?"

"Yeah, but the parents have lawyered up, and I can't get them to answer anything."

"I hate lawyers and assholes who hide behind them," I stated forcefully.

"It's their prerogative, and I would probably do the same in their situation," Sam replied.

"Maybe so, but is there a way to get a meeting through the lawyer?"

"We've done that. The DA is negotiating terms as we speak."

"Not good enough," I said. "What if I try to catch Tommy after school to see if he would chat with me?"

"I can't stop you, but I can't endorse it either. If you do, make sure to tell me what you learn."

"You got it Sam. See you soon."

I told Lee where I was going, and drove to Madisonville High School, home to the mighty Fire Ants. I always laughed at their mascot, until I stepped in a fire ant bed. That's not a laughing matter, I assure you.

I checked the parking lot and found a black Toyota Tacoma. Hoping it was Tommy's truck, I parked nearby and waited.

Tommy walked right by me, with neither of us knowing the other. When he stopped at the truck, I stepped up near him. "Tommy?" He looked at me, nodding slightly. I stuck my hand out, introducing myself and reminded him about speaking with me on the phone.

"Are you and Michael okay? I hate that talking to me got you guys into an argument."

He laughed, "We're good. Just a misunderstanding, that's all."

I smiled, "Glad to hear it. I felt really bad about it, so I wanted to stop by and apologize."

"No worries, you sure didn't need to do that, but thanks."

I shook his hand and turned to go, acting as if the meeting were ended. Before I had gone more than two steps, I stopped and turned back to ask, "Hey, do you know what Gary's friend's name is? You know, the guy up in Franklinton?"

Tommy looked confused, "Don't know which one you're talking about. He's got a couple of hunting buddies up there."

"I think I remember he owned some land, or a business or something." It sounded so vague and terrible, I figured Tommy wouldn't bite. But he did, "You must be talking about Cory, he owns the body shop there."

"I think you're right," I smiled. "Thanks, and sorry again about the phone call." Sometimes luck does favor the bold.

When I reached my car, I looked around to make sure nobody was watching and side-kicked the front panel of my car, leaving a nice dent. It looked like I needed some auto body work. *Oh, where should I go?* I made myself laugh at times.

Google revealed there were three body shops in Franklinton. I hit pay dirt on the second call, when I asked for Cory. "This is Cory, how may I help you?" he asked, speaking with a heavy hillbilly accent.

"Hi, I've got a dented quarter panel. A friend of mine told me to call you to check it out. He said you guys do good work at a reasonable price, and I don't want to turn it in to my insurance."

"No problem, you want to come in today for me to give it a once over?"

"That'd be great," I replied. "I can be there in an hour."

"See you then," Cory said. "Make sure to ask for me."

"I surely will, thank you."

I called Lee to get everything he could on the body shop, and Cory in particular. I then called Sam to give him the information. He advised me to play it easy. I told him I was going to look around to see if I saw either Gary or the Camaro. I didn't tell him I was going to ask about Gary if I didn't see anything. There was no point in getting another lecture from Sam.

Lee texted me the information about the shop and our friend Cory Aucoin, so I was ready by the time I made it to the location. At the counter was a large, and by 'large' I mean both tall and fat, man who looked to be around 30 years old. I asked for Cory, and he stuck out his hand.

"I'm Cory, are you the lady with the dented fender?"

I took the meaty paw in my hand, feeling how strong he was. "That's me. I'm Jessie. Can you come out and take a look at the damage?"

"Sure thing. Let me get my iPad to write up the estimate."

He went into an office and left me alone. He returned quickly enough that I didn't have time to look around. I led him outside to the damaged panel. Giving it a glance, he asked what happened.

"I don't know. I came out from the store and saw it. I guess someone hit me in the parking lot," I added.

"Don't see any paint on it, so it looks more like someone kicked it or fell into it." He pointed at the dent, continuing, "See how the paint isn't scratched? If it were hit by something metal, the paint would have scratched or chipped."

"That makes sense," I said, realizing this guy knew his shit. "Hey, is it okay if I use your bathroom while you write the estimate?"

"Sure, it's inside to the right," he said motioning with his hand. I went inside to have a look around. The main shop area had four bays for cars to be worked on, and another section that was closed off. I guessed that was for painting. All the bays had cars, with three of them being actively worked on. The fourth bay held a blue car, and as I got closer, I realized it was a Camaro. There was no front plate on the car, so I walked behind it and snapped a quick picture with my phone. I then went to the restroom and pulled up the picture. I compared the number to the one Sam had texted me, but it wasn't a match.

Returning to my car, Cory appeared to be done. He was smiling when I approached.

"Well Miss Jessie, this dent is one we can pull out. We don't have to do much to it, and I don't think the paint will be affected. It should be nice and easy. The estimate, if that's all we have to do, is only $200."

"Seems reasonable to me," I said. "When can you do it, and how long will it take?"

"Job like this can be done in a couple of hours so we can do it almost any day. When would you like to bring it in?"

"Tell you what, let me check my work schedule when I get home and I'll call to make an appointment," I suggested.

"That's fine. Thanks for thinking about us," He smiled, shaking my hand again.

Driving away, I called Sam to give him the disappointing news. When I told him about the blue Camaro, he hesitated, then asked, "What's the plate number? If they painted the car a new color, they may have also changed the plate."

I hadn't thought about that, but it was a possibility. I gave him the number so he could pull the DMV records on it. He told me he'd call right back. True to his word, the phone rang less than five minutes later.

"Any luck?" I answered.

"Very much so. That plate is registered to a 1997 Cadillac, not to a Camaro."

"Holy shit, Gary may have been there," I said. "How are you going to play this?"

"I'm not going to dick around with it. I've already got a team on the way. We're working with the local Sheriff and we're going to hit it hard and fast. Need to make sure if he's there, he doesn't get away. I just left the office and will be there in 30 minutes give or take. Make sure you're not close by when it goes down."

I confirmed I would keep my distance, but I wasn't going anywhere until I knew if Gary was at the shop. I took up position at a coffee house less than a block away, but with a good line of sight. Only a few more minutes passed before a bevy of vehicles converged. They'd been running silently, which made sense since they wouldn't want Gary to bolt.

Men jumped out of every vehicle, armed to the teeth. Orders were shouted by the officers causing the employees to come spilling into the parking lot, where they were corralled and ushered to a holding area behind the vehicles. Two heavily armed guards stood watch over them as a team rushed into the building.

I didn't hear any shots thankfully. Less than 10 minutes later, a group of policemen came out with a man in cuffs. Big guy, black hair: Gary. I paid for the coffee and walked to the security tape that was now in place around the parking lot. Officials were going through their business efficiently and professionally. I suspect this was the A team.

I finally saw Sam and waved to him. He nodded, then turned his back to me to speak with an officer. I could see Gary in the back of a police car, being secured for transport to the station. What I didn't see was a 14-year-old girl. My heart began to sink, realizing Madison was most likely dead.

Sam walked to me with a stern look. Before I could say anything, he stated, "Don't ask. I can't tell you anything other than nobody seems to know where Madison is. The employees all deny having ever seen her and Gary isn't talking. He wants a lawyer."

"Can we get dogs to the camp now?" I asked.

"Already requested," he confirmed.

"Search dogs or cadaver dogs?" I cringed even as I asked.

"Both," came the grim reply.

The drive home went by unnoticed as my mind was working on what to tell Alice. I had to tell her Gary had been found and he wasn't talking, but I wasn't so sure about anything else. In the end, I decided I would be honest with her. I drove straight to their house, hoping she was home.

Michael answered the door and confirmed Alice was home. She quickly came out, a nervous expression outlining her face. "Hi Alice, we've made some progress," I started. She waited for me to continue.

I gave her the basics, wrapping up with the arrest and the fact that nobody admitted to seeing Madison.

"So, what's next?" Alice asked, resignation in her voice. She knew there would not be a happy ending.

"There's some property Gary leases for hunting. The police are sending search dogs to see if they can pick up a scent." Tears started streaming down Alice's face, and mine quickly followed. I stepped in and hugged her with all my might, having no words to help ease her pain.

We hugged for the longest time, sobs wracking us both. Michael came out and saw us, before lowering his head and going back to his room. In a weird, out-of-body experience, I wondered how Michael and Tommy were going to get along if Cory did in fact kill Madison Everyone in this situation was fucked.

When we finally broke the embrace, Alice looked at me and said, "I'm not stupid. I know this means Madison is probably dead, but there's a chance she's alive, isn't there?"

I didn't want to give her false hope, but technically she was right. Until we found a body, there was always a chance. "There is Alice, and I will pray that's the case. Do you want me to stay with you a while, or would you prefer me to leave?"

"Can you stay until Dale gets here?" I nodded as she went in the other room to call Dale. Dale arrived quickly, Alice explained what had happened, and I answered a few questions for Dale before taking my leave. I cried again on my way home, not knowing how I was possibly going to process all of this.

CHAPTER 7

Gary's capture and arrest triggered a whirlwind of activity. He was being held without bail on kidnapping charges, but I was sure many more charges would be added as the investigation unfolded. He remained tight-lipped, refusing to say anything at all to investigators. Sam assured me the DA was doing everything possible to pressure Gary into revealing the whereabouts of Madison. His lawyer continued to assert the 5th amendment on behalf of his client.

It was noon the next day when Sam called to tell me they had found a body. From appearances, it matched Madison's description. It was buried in a shallow grave about a half mile from the camp. Sam couldn't answer most of my questions, but he confirmed the body was being taken to the coroner for an autopsy. He also told me there was a jurisdictional fight between St. Tammany Parish where the kidnapping occurred, and Washington Parish where the death occurred. As far as I was concerned, they each should get their shot at Gary.

The final piece of information Sam shared was that the family had been called to identify the body. I knew I needed to call, though dreaded doing so. I wanted to be strong for Alice but wasn't feeling sure of myself. Nevertheless, as soon as I hung up with Sam, I called Alice. She answered calmly, "Hello?" I figured she must either be in denial or shock.

"Hi Alice, it's Jess. I just heard the news from Detective Arnold. I'm so sorry." I didn't really know what to tell a woman who just found out her daughter was dead.

"Thanks, Dale is on the way to identify the body."

"You're welcome, I just wish there was something else I could have done," I said, thinking about what I'd do if Gary escaped justice.

"Nothing you could have done would have changed the outcome. I know that," she said with resignation. After a pause, she asked, "Can I ask you a few questions?"

"Sure, I'll answer anything I can," I replied, hoping to be of some help during this time of grief.

"What's going to happen to Madison now?"

"Once the identity has been confirmed, they will then conduct an autopsy. The goal is to determine what caused Madison's death so the District Attorney can file appropriate charges against Gary. This may take a while depending on how long it takes to get back blood tests which are sent out to a lab." I didn't feel it necessary to mention DNA testing that will be involved.

I switched the phone to my other ear as I continued, "Once the autopsy is complete, they will release Madison to you for her funeral. You won't have to do anything, other than have the funeral home notified. They will make the transportation arrangements."

"Do they have to do an autopsy? I hate the thought of them cutting her up. It just makes me sick to my stomach," she said, starting to cry.

"I'm afraid the law requires it in all circumstances of questionable death. And without it, we would never know what caused her to die. That would be bad, because if Gary killed her, the evidence gathered during the autopsy will be crucial to convicting him."

"I guess I already knew that, I just hate it."

"I understand. Is there anything else I can answer for you?"

"Yes, what's going to happen to Gary?"

I knew this question was coming and had my answer ready to go. "He will be held in jail without bail until all the charges have been brought. The District Attorney will use the evidence found by the police and the coroner to determine what charges are appropriate. A grand jury will hear the evidence from the DA and issue an indictment for any charges that are supported by the evidence. Once indicted, the case will take a while, so please don't expect everything to resolve quickly."

"What do you think Gary will be charged with?" Alice interrupted.

"I can't really say for sure. If we assume he killed her, he will be charged with murder, either first degree which means he planned it, or second degree which means he did it, but didn't plan it ahead of time. He will also be charged with other crimes as evidence comes out." I didn't want to talk about rape right now. It wouldn't do any good to upset her further.

I finished by saying, "I think it's safe to say Gary will either spend the rest of his life in jail or get the death penalty."

Alice didn't respond at first, but when she did, it was almost a whisper. "I hope he rots in jail forever. I want him to be beat and raped for years for what he did to Madison." I shared her sentiment; Gary deserved as much pain as could possibly be delivered.

I offered to do anything the family needed to support them. Alice thanked me and hung up. I looked dully at the phone and realized my heart was broken.

The next few days passed in a fog. Dad called me for lunch. We met even though I wasn't in the mood. He asked what was going on, and I gave him the basics. It was a quiet lunch after that. I wasn't ready to talk about it, and Dad was smart enough not to push me.

Back at work, I did what I needed to do for my other cases, but everything seemed to move in slow motion. I bugged Sam almost every day about the autopsy results. It was a week after Madison was found when Sam finally told me what I wanted to know.

"Hi Sam, how are you?"

"Busy and angry, how about you?" he replied.

"I'm okay," I said, knowing any other answer may lead me into a discussion I didn't want to have. "Any word yet?"

"I finally got the verbal report on the autopsy today. The coroner is putting together the final report, but it's bad."

"Give it all to me," I replied. "Don't leave anything out."

"Better take a seat," He cautioned. I was already seated, but steeled myself for the news.

"Go ahead," I growled.

"Cause of death was a heart attack. The heart attack was brought on by an overdose of a mixture of drugs. She tested positive for marijuana, crystal meth and even heroin. There were significant signs of sexual trauma, both vaginal and anal. She had rope burns on both wrists and around her neck." I started to feel nauseous during Sam's recitation of the findings. I cut him off so I could catch my breath.

"When did she die?"

"The coroner estimates she died approximately 48 hours before we found her."

I counted the days, "If my math is correct, she was being drugged, raped and tortured for about 5 days, right?"

"That's our best guess as well," he acknowledged.

A deep breath calmed my exterior, but inside, my blood boiled into a rage. I swore to myself at that moment that Gary Bordelon was going to die in agony. Once I decided his fate, a cold calmness ran through me.

"Does the family know?" I asked.

"No, they won't hear anything until the official report is finalized."

"Has the DA questioned Gary based on the findings?"

"Gary's lawyer was given the basics, but Gary is still refusing to talk."

"When he does talk, can I see the video, or at least get a transcript of the interview?"

"That won't be public record, Jess. You know that."

"I need it Sam, I need to see it," I said with as much control as I could muster.

He understood my need, and confirmed it when he said, "I'll do what I can."

In Louisiana, first degree murder can be charged when death is also connected with other violent felonies. The list includes aggravated and second-degree kidnapping, cruelty to juveniles and aggravated or forcible rape. Since all these applied, I believed it was clearly a first-degree murder case.

Louisiana has the death penalty, meaning Gary was looking at death by lethal injection. Of course, it would likely take 20 years or more.

Knowing all of this, I asked, "The DA already tell the defendant he will be charged with first degree murder?"

"Yes, but he's offered to reduce it to second degree or statutory rape, and agree to a twenty-year sentence if the defendant pleads guilty," Sam said quietly.

"Wait, what?!" I screamed into the phone.

"Don't take it out on me," Sam pushed back. "That's just what I heard."

"Why would he possibly offer that?" I asked, my voice still loud.

"You know he's running for re-election and if he gets a quick guilty plea, he can focus his time and energy on his campaign. At least, that's my opinion," Sam offered.

I didn't say another word, I simply hung up.

Sitting at my desk, I made my plan. It was simple, efficient and would result in Dale screaming in agony. I nodded, smiled to myself and then dismissed the mother fucker from my thoughts.

Two weeks to the day from my call with Sam, I was sitting in the courtroom for Gary's arraignment. The list of charges was read to all, and if Gary were tried on those charges, he would most certainly be convicted. The evidence was overwhelming.

Sam had called a few days before to tell me the interview had finally taken place. He refused to provide me with either the video or a transcript, but his summary was enough.

Gary claimed Madison was a druggie who voluntarily took all the drugs. She was also a sex fiend, wanting it day and night. He knew he shouldn't have sex with a minor, but between the drugs and her seduction, he was weak and had sex with her.

When asked about the rope burns, Gary claimed Madison was into some kinky shit and loved being tied up. As for the shallow grave burial, Gary was terribly sorry, but he freaked out when she overdosed, and he made a mistake.

Sam confirmed Gary had been well coached by his lawyer, making sure to sow the seeds for a plea deal.

Back in the courtroom, the judge asked the defendant if he understood the charges. Gary confirmed he did. The judge asked how he pled, and Gary plead not guilty before sitting down.

The District Attorney asked the judge for a sidebar, with both lawyers speaking quietly to the judge. The judge finally nodded, sending the attorneys back to their respective seats.

The judge looked to the audience, and said, "The District Attorney and defense attorney have agreed to a plea bargain. The terms set forth are the defendant will plead guilty to statutory rape, and in exchange, all other charges will be dropped. The District Attorney has recommended a sentence of twenty years in prison. The defendant has agreed to these terms."

The Judge removed his glasses, and rubbed his hand across his face before continuing, "The court is not bound by this agreement, however. We will go into recess to allow me time to review the case and issue a ruling on the plea deal. Court adjourned," he said while banging the gavel.

The crowd erupted in confusion, and I saw Alice bury her head in her hands, crying her eyes out. I quickly stepped into the hall, along the route where Gary would be escorted out. Security was tight, but I waited for the exact right time, slipping through and bumping into the defendant. He looked at me as I clearly said the word, "Pain," making sure he was the only one that could hear me. He looked at me in confusion. I smiled as I was pushed aside, and Gary was hustled out of the building. All the while, he was still looking back at me. My job had been done.

The court reconvened later in the day. I wasn't there, so didn't hear the judge announce he was accepting the plea deal. It mattered not to me because Gary was a walking dead man. He just didn't know it yet.

CHAPTER 8

Late the next morning, I was at my desk thinking about the mistake I made. I should never had made myself noticeable when exacting my vengeance on Gary. I'd never done it before and vowed to never do it again. My existence rested on being in the shadows, unknown to anyone.

I was expecting a phone call, and surprised that it hadn't come in yet. I suspected I would hear word of Gary's condition soon enough though, so I opened my laptop to review a report Lee had compiled for me on another case.

It was no surprise when Sam called me thirty minutes later. The conversation didn't go as expected though. "Good morning, Sam," I answered cheerily.

"Not really," Sam sounded aggravated.

"What's going on?" I asked, playing dumb.

"Before I get into it, I want to know what the fuck that was yesterday. Why'd you break through security and confront Gary?"

"I didn't 'confront' him, I simply had to look him in the eyes after all I'd gone through trying to find Madison," I replied as angrily as I thought I could get away with.

"That's amateur hour bullshit!" Now his voice was rising. "As long as I've known you, I've never seen you shit the bed like you did yesterday." He continued, "Everyone knows about our relationship, and you're making my job a lot harder by pulling a stunt like that. And you did it even after all the help I gave you." He wasn't done yet, so I let him get it out. "It's like you spit in my face," he finished, his voice finally dying down.

I hadn't considered this when I planned the execution and cursed myself for being short-sighted. "I'm really sorry Sam. I'd never do anything intentionally to hurt you. I just let my emotions get away from me. I promise I'll never let that happen again." I didn't want to burn such a valuable resource, and more importantly, I didn't want to hurt someone whom I loved very much.

"I'm sorry I yelled at you, but there's been an unexpected turn of events."

I thought I knew where this was going but needed to make sure. "What's happened?" I asked.

"Gary was brought to the hospital this morning in severe pain. He screamed all night, but the duty officer just thought he was trying to get out of his cell by pretending. Turns out, he really was in horrible pain. They found him unconscious during the early morning rounds. When he was roused, he just screamed until he passed out again."

I listened carefully, hoping Gary was thinking about the pain he caused Madison as he endured the worst pain in his life. After a pause, Sam continued, "They ran some tests before taking him into surgery. We don't know what it is right now."

I certainly wasn't going to educate Sam. "Sounds like Karma came a calling," I replied.

"Maybe, but the son-of-a-bitch better not die. We still have to interview him about the woman's shoe we found," came his response.

"Why?" He caught me flat-footed.

"We asked his family and none of them owned that shoe. That means there could be another victim of his depravity out there somewhere, and if he dies, we will never find out."

Fuck...fuck...fuck

"Can't you interview him in the hospital when he comes out of surgery?"

"No way, his lawyer will never allow it. He'll be heavily medicated and nothing he says could be counted on. I just hope whatever he has isn't life threatening."

It's 99% fatal...fuck

I had nothing to offer, so after asking Sam to keep me updated, I hung up. What if Gary had drugged, raped or killed another girl? I tried to console myself with the fact he would never own up to it, but I sure as hell removed any possibility he might. It seemed my decision making was going from bad to worse.

Several hours later I was told Gary was terminal with a dead bowel. The medical term for this is intestinal ischemia. It's caused by loss of blood flow to the intestines, usually through a clot. When the blood flow is completely blocked off, the intestine dies and can quickly become gangrenous. If caught quickly, surgery can be performed to save the patient's life. Once the tissue dies and infection is widespread though, surgery is unable to correct the situation.

As Gary was screaming all night in pain, his blockage would not have been addressed quickly enough to save his life. Like I said earlier, he was a dead man walking.

Gary never regained consciousness, passing away the next day. I was again at the office when I was informed. I'd done what I set out to do, but may have hurt another family in the process. Looking for some validation, I called Alice to inform her.

When she answered, I jumped straight in. "Did you hear Gary died today? He went to the hospital and they tried surgery, but they couldn't save him."

"I heard," was all she said.

I'd have thought she would have seemed happy, but she didn't at all. I decided to up the ante a little bit. "I heard he was screaming all night in his cell. He must have been in terrible pain, and I can't say I'm sorry to hear it," I said, opening the door for her to express her satisfaction.

"So what? He had some pain for a day? My Madison suffered for almost a week. I wanted him to suffer for years for what he did!" She was now screaming.

This had totally blown up in my face, and there was no way to salvage it. "I'm sorry to have troubled you, I just wanted to make sure you heard." Alice didn't even reply before disconnecting.

I put my head down on the desk, crying uncontrollably. When I gathered myself together, I told Lee I was going home for the day. I got home, crawled in bed and cried again until sleep took me.

It was early evening when I woke up, feeling somewhat better. I needed company, and no one was better company than Becky. I called her to see if she wanted to get a few drinks. Unfortunately, she and her boyfriend had plans for the evening. She invited me to tag along, but I wasn't in the mood to be a third wheel, so I passed.

I showered, put on makeup and a cute summer dress before making a cocktail. Deciding drinking alone wasn't going to help me, I pulled out my phone and set up a Tinder account. Snapping a quick picture, my profile was completed. I logged in to see who was near me.

I had fun swiping through, seeing the guys who were available. One of them looked quite handsome, having beautiful eyes and a great smile. Maybe it was Steve's lucky night. I swiped right and was almost immediately notified Steve matched with me. We communicated and agreed to meet at a bar down the street from my place.

Steve was seated with a beer when I arrived. In person, he looked as good as his profile pic. It was also evident he worked out. He was muscular, but not bulky. I sure hoped his personality matched his appearance.

We chatted, got to know each other a bit and had a few drinks. I didn't drink too much though, wanting to make sure I didn't get myself into a dangerous situation. After an hour, Steve suggested we go to someplace more private. I was game and we ended up choosing his place for the night.

The next morning, I called Becky. "Well, I did it," I opened the conversation.

"What is 'it'?" she laughed.

"Tinder."

"Nooo, really?" Her incredulousness was obvious.

"I sure did. Really sexy man named Steve."

"How did it go?" she asked.

"Eh, nice time at the bar, but once we went back to his place, it was five minutes of foreplay and two minutes of sex. I should've just stayed home and taken care of things myself."

"Well, that sucks," she said. "Did you exchange numbers? Maybe he'd be better the next time."

"I took his number, but I'm not going to call. I really wasn't into him. As good as he looked, I think he's probably lacking somewhat in intelligence."

"You were safe, right?"

"Yes, I'm not stupid you know."

"Good," Becky said with finality. "Hey, you remember telling me to go to my doctor?"

I did but hadn't thought about it again with everything that had been happening. "Yeah, did you go?"

"Yes. They did an ultrasound and found some nodules on both sides of my thyroid. They're going to do a needle biopsy this week to see if it's cancer."

I nodded to myself, "I'm really happy you went. Catching it early means you have a huge likelihood of full remission and leading a normal life. I love you, Becky."

"Thanks for making me go. I owe you one," she replied. Before I could suggest she buy the next round of drinks, she added, "Now your turn, have you gone to see a professional?"

"No, but I need some help. Did you hear about my client?"

"I did, I'm sorry she was killed like that. I also heard the perp had a terrible death himself."

"Looks that way, but everyone is pissed. He may have been involved in some other shit, so the police are disappointed they didn't get to interview him more. And my client wanted him to rot in jail for years, so she thinks he got off easy." I sighed before continuing, "As for me, I'm glad he suffered, but am sorry everyone else is suffering also."

It was clear Becky didn't know what to say. All she could offer was, "You need to talk with someone."

I agreed before we made plans to have lunch the next day. All day I pondered who I could go see. Any professional I saw would be legally bound to report my illegal activities. If I tried to keep that information out of the discussion, I would be defeating the purpose. The executions were exactly what I needed to talk about. No good solution came to mind.

Driving through downtown Madisonville, I passed the Holy Trinity Catholic Church. I'd seen it many times in the past, if only noticing the beautiful building. And like a thunderclap, it hit me. I could speak with a priest in the confessional. Not being Catholic might be an obstacle, but I was going to stop and ask anyway.

I parked in the empty lot and walked into the chapel. I saw one person seated in a pew, praying with rosary in hand. Nobody else was visible so I walked around the building. I finally spied a man wearing a black shirt and a white clerical collar. He appeared to be in his thirties and was walking my direction with a smooth, measured gait. As he approached, I introduced myself.

"Hello, Father. My name is Jessie Edwards. Would you have a moment to answer some questions?" I tried not to look desperate, but suspected I was failing.

"Pleased to meet you Ms. Edwards. I am Father Grayson. What can I do for you?" He asked, while extending his hand for me to shake.

Taking a deep breath, I plunged in. "I'm not Catholic, I was raised Presbyterian, but I have a great need to confess my sins."

He looked intently into my eyes, almost as if he were reading my mind. "I see. Not being Catholic though means you are not allowed to receive the sacrament of confession. May I ask why you would come to us?"

"What I need to confess can never be shared, and I believed the secrecy of the confessional is absolute in the Catholic Church. Am I correct about that?"

"For all intents and purposes, yes. In some circumstances, I could consult with another person, such as a bishop for guidance. But even if I were to do so, I would not reveal the person's name or anything that could be used to identify them."

"That's the answer to your question, Father. I need absolute secrecy."

"Would you like to come to my office?" he asked, sweeping his hand down the hallway.

"Does everything we discuss there have the same privacy as the confessional?"

He shook his head, "No, it does not."

I was getting more desperate by the moment, "Father, I've committed sins of a terrible nature, and I need to find a private way in which to relieve myself of this burden."

He looked thoughtfully at me. "In 2016, Pope Francis led a global 'confession drive'. During that time, the Church encouraged non-Catholics to speak in strict confidence to a priest about problems in their lives. The privacy associated with traditional confession was given to non-Catholics as part of this drive. The goal was to offer a similar experience of unburdening oneself that Catholics receive as part of the sacrament of confession. The main difference was non-Catholics would not actually be participating in the sacrament. This meant they would not go through the formal steps of expressing penitence for their sins. People would also not receive absolution, but would receive a blessing at the end of the session."

I asked hopefully, "Is there any way I can avail myself of this program, even though it isn't in place right now?"

He considered for a moment. "Please stay here. I would like to call my bishop to seek his guidance." He waved me to a chair and disappeared down the hall towards his office. I don't know how long he was gone, but it seemed an eternity. I was close to leaving when he reappeared, striding purposefully down the hall.

"I've received permission to allow you to participate in the experience," he said with a smile. "Please follow me."

Once we were seated in the confessional booth, with the screen dividing us, I asked, "How does this work?'

"Generally, the person confessing starts by saying, 'Father, forgive me for I have sinned.' They then tell me how long it's been since their last confession and start by confessing their mortal sins. If they don't have any mortal sins, they will confess their venial sins. Based on what you've told me, I'm guessing you want to confess your mortal sins. Since this isn't the sacrament though, you can start however you like and tell me about whatever is troubling you"

I nodded before realizing he really couldn't see me "Right, so here we go. Father, I have killed people." I couldn't believe the words were coming out of my mouth, but they were, and once they started, I didn't filter them at all.

"I've killed nine people over the past five years. I killed them when they escaped justice for the horrible crimes they committed. These people were rapists and murderers, the most evil of people. They preyed on the weak and used their power and money to avoid convictions. I refused to let them get away, leaving devastation in their wake, so I became their judge, juror and executioner."

A long silence followed. Long enough that I wondered if I'd made another terrible decision. Father Grayson finally said, "What gives you the right to judge these people?"

"I've thought about that many times, Father. I don't have the right, I know that. But, if I did nothing when it was in my power to do so, I would feel complicit in their crimes."

"How are you able to kill without being caught?"

I wasn't ready to share that information, so I generalized. "I have unique abilities that help me avoid detection. Well, at least so far they have."

Again, there was a pause before Father Grayson, said, "The fifth commandment says, 'Thou shall not kill.' And Romans 12:19 tells us the Lord says, 'Vengeance is mine, I will repay.' As a Christian, why do you not follow His words?"

"I know I'm not being a good Christian. And not one of these criminals took an action that was personal to me. But I've watched our criminal justice system fail for years. It fails the people who are the least fortunate, and those who are the least able to defend themselves. To me, it's unacceptable to not use the abilities God gave to me."

"What abilities are you referring to?" He asked.

Again, I wasn't ready to answer that question. "That'll have to be for another day, Father."

"How do you decide which people deserve to die?"

"I have a set of rules I follow, I guess kind of like the Ten Commandments. The first is the criminal justice system must be allowed to run its course. The second is I must be one hundred percent sure the person is guilty. The third is I will never execute a minor, no matter how bad their crime. My fourth rule is the execution must be as soon as possible after their subversion of justice. I refuse to give these people any chance to harm another living being. My last rule is I should perform the execution in as painless a manner as possible."

"God's the only one who has the right to judge us," he replied.

"And it's my goal to get those people to God as fast as I can so He can judge them."

"Are you truly asking for forgiveness? If you are, have you decided you will never kill another person?"

"That's the million-dollar question, Father. I've told myself I'd stop in the past, only to be presented with a new case involving a truly deserving person, and I find myself doing it all over again."

Father Grayson considered my answers before asking his next question. "Why did you come here today? Specifically, today? Something must have happened to bring you here."

He was quite insightful it seemed. "I broke my number one rule when I executed the last person; I didn't let the criminal justice system work. I was so devasted by the way he drugged, raped and murdered a 14-year-old girl, I killed him the moment I had a chance."

"I see." He followed up the comment with, "You're talking about the Reynold's girl, aren't you?"

I froze, knowing I'd given him too much information. I couldn't lie at this point though, so I weakly said, "Yes."

"The family is part of our congregation. I knew Madison well and will miss her." I could hear sorrow and pain in his voice.

"I didn't know her, but I do know what Gary Bordelon did to her, and it's brutal. Do you want me to give you the details?" I asked, trying to shock him into seeing things my way.

"That's not necessary," was his simple reply. "Do you have anything else you'd like to confess?"

"No, Father. I know I've sinned in many other ways, but I'm comfortable speaking directly to God about those sins."

"I'm not sure you're sorrowful for your sins, and you haven't resolved to avoid sinning in the future. Based on this, if you were Catholic, I would be unable to absolve you of your sins. Since you aren't Catholic, I can give still you a blessing though. Please close your eyes and receive this blessing." I did as instructed.

"Oh, merciful Lord, please guide Jessie Edwards in her life. Please show her your will and help break her away from this vicious cycle she has set herself upon. Your mercies and love are boundless, and I beg thee to bring Ms. Edwards to the side of all that is good and righteous. In Jesus' name we pray, Amen."

"Amen," I said. "Would I be permitted to see you in the confessional again?"

"Absolutely. I want to bring you back to the path of righteousness. I will do whatever is in my power to help you, but I won't ever be able to absolve you of your sins."

"Thank you, Father." And with that, I left.

CHAPTER 9

The next month passed uneventfully. I had my regular visit with Mom, lunches with Dad and Becky and all was seemingly normal. The nightmares were absent the entire time, work returned to routine, as did my exercise and other daily rituals.

The weather finally started to cool, leaving me with the desire to be outside more often. When the weather was nice, the lakefront was always one of my favorite places to jog. One Friday evening, I felt the urge to run. I drove to the lake, parking in the marina lot. I set off at a brisk pace along the paved pathway, loving every minute of being outdoors.

The sun set midway through my run and the temperature dropped noticeably. I picked up the pace, wanting to get back to the car before it got too cold. I reached a bend in the path where a giant oak tree stood. A man stepped out from behind the oak and stood directly in my line. He looked to be in his twenties, lean and wiry. In his right hand was a large knife.

I stopped and raised my hands to hopefully calm down the situation. He didn't say anything, he just looked at me.

"I don't carry any money when I run," I said.

"Then we'll have to make do with something else," he leered at me and stepped forward. Two steps in, he stopped, dropped the knife and grabbed for his throat, clearly struggling to breathe. Falling to his knees, he fell over unconscious within 30 seconds. By this time, he was flat on his back, legs splayed open. I walked up to him and planted two powerful kicks to his groin. The first he deserved. The second was just because I wanted to.

I reached into my fanny pack, pulled out my phone and called Sam. I told him what happened, where I was, and asked that he send a car to pick up the suspect. Two minutes later, sirens wailed, and two police cars came screeching to a halt. Officers hustled over to me, while I leaned against the oak tree watching the still unconscious mugger.

Two officers secured the knife, cuffed my assailant, and dragged him to their car. Another was taking my statement when Sam arrived. I told them everything that happened, leaving out the ball busting of course. Sam stood and listened to me answer questions about the event. When the officer was done, Sam pulled me to one side.

"Sounds like you got lucky, Jess."

"I guess so. I would've used my kickboxing skills if push had come to shove, but I'm much happier he passed out. Maybe he's on drugs or something." With a devious smile, I added, "If he wakes up complaining about his nuts hurting, it absolutely has nothing to do with me planting my foot up his crotch a couple of times."

Sam laughed, "I'd expect nothing less." He then took a more serious tone, "You really shouldn't be out running by yourself like this after dark."

I checked my initial retort and said, "I guess I didn't realize how late it was and how far I'd run. I'll definitely be more careful going forward."

He smiled, "Good, I'd hate to lose you to some piece of shit like that guy."

"Won't happen," I assured him. Changing gears, I asked, "It's been a while since we've talked, how have you been?"

He shook his head, "Jackie broke up with me last week. Said me being a cop was too hard on the relationship."

"Damn, I'm sorry. I know you love her a lot."

"Yeah, something must be wrong with me since you ladies keep leaving me."

Again, I felt that pang in my chest. Against my better judgement, I asked, "Why don't we get a bite to eat tomorrow? We can catch up and tell each other our tales of sorrow."

"I'd like that. Usual place at 7pm?" He asked.

"See you there," I replied with a smile.

I was called into the police station the next morning to give my statement again. I assured them I would testify against the mugger when time came. At the station, I asked if anyone had determined what had happened to the mugger. I was told he regained consciousness in the car and claimed he had been choked. I laughed that off and went about my day.

When Sam and I were dating, we had a favorite dive restaurant we'd go to for seafood and drinks. I was seated there sipping a beer when Sam arrived.

He gave me a hug, saying, "You look nice."

"Thanks. Lots of sleep and exercise have been good for me."

Sitting down, we casually chatted until our orders were taken and Sam got his beer. Taking his first sip, he moved to more serious topics. "How have you been since Madison's death?"

Quite a few emotions coursed through me at the same time. I knew Sam well enough to not brush off the question. "It was rough for a while. I kept asking myself what I could've done to find her faster, but eventually I realized there was nothing I would have changed. I accepted that it wasn't my fault and I'd done everything I could. That made it a lot easier for me to sleep at night." I paused briefly before adding, "Yeah, that and talking to a priest."

Sam gave me the cutest quizzical look I'd ever seen. "A priest? You're not Catholic, so what's that about?"

"Seems weird I know, but I was driving by the church right after we found Madison. I was totally in a fog and just knew I had to speak with someone. Father Grayson was nice enough to listen to me for a long time. All I can say is confession is good for the soul."

"How'd you go to confession with you not being Catholic?"

Oops. "It's a figure of speech, Sam. I just meant it helped to talk things out with someone."

"Kind of like what we're doing tonight?" he asked.

"Kind of," I said, while thinking, *but not really.*

The meal was delicious as always. Spending time with Sam felt like going home. Going home for a visit, more precisely; I knew I'd never be able to move home again.

I asked about his breakup with Jackie. He spoke at length about how his hours and her fears led them to end the relationship. It's not everyone who can live with a cop.

At the end of the evening, Sam asked if we could do this again. Alarm bells went off in my head, but my big mouth betrayed me when I said, "Of course. I'd like that."

A week later, we were together again, and all seemed right in the world. Things were wonderful for another month, until a fateful Wednesday. I was at the office, on the phone with Sam. He interrupted our conversation.

"Sorry, Jess. Got to go. I just got word a man we've been looking for was seen."

"Sure thing. Be safe," I replied.

"Love you," he said and disconnected. I didn't have the chance to tell him I loved him too.

For me, all that was good and pure in my life was destroyed that day. A humble, kind, loving man was taken from both the world and from me.

Sam and his partner went to a house where they had been told the suspect was holed up. Both had taken the precaution of wearing their vests. The man they had been looking for was wanted in connection with a drug ring operating in southeast Louisiana.

According to his partner, Sam knocked on the door and announced himself to be a police officer. The door opened and immediately a shotgun blasted in Sam's face. He never had a chance and was dead before he hit the ground.

Sam's partner pulled his pistol and returned fire, but the suspect barricaded himself in the house. It took a police negotiator long hours to convince the killer to give up. Thankfully, nobody else was injured in the process. The story made national news for several days, at least until another tragedy redirected everyone's attention.

The killer was held in the parish jail without bail. I learned the killer's name was Eric Peterman.

He was eventually charged with first degree murder, along with other irrelevant charges. Killing a cop might make him a big deal in prison, but since it was my cop he killed, the odds of him surviving too long were negligible.

The nightmares returned the night Sam died. Along with the 11th birthday recurring dream, a new nightmare was added to the mix. In this one, I dreamed I was in a church. There was a minister preaching, but the only other people in the pews were my victims. Sam was the exception. He was also there, sitting at the end of my pew, simply staring at me. As the preacher spoke about love and kindness, one after another of my victims started spewing blood from their orifices. Screams and moans filled the church, but the preacher kept going as if nothing were happening. Horrified, I looked at Sam, and he just stared at me before getting up and walking out.

For weeks thereafter, that nightmare dominated my waking hours and my dreams. Restful sleep became more and more rare, and my mood darkened commensurately.

About a month after Sam was killed, I woke from the nightmare and decided it was time for JJE to return. 'Vengeance is mine,' sayeth the Lord. But He was going to have to get in line behind me. I was going to make a visit to the parish jail.

This turned out to be a more difficult task than I imagined. In order to get to see Peterman, I needed to be on his approved visitor list. Since I wasn't, I needed him to add me.

I mailed a letter to Peterman at the prison. I knew all mail would be checked so I was cautious with my wording. In the letter, I explained that I was a private investigator and had been asked to consult on a fiction novel. The main character in the book was a drug mule. I asked Peterman to add me to his visitor list so I could use him as a resource for how a drug mule worked. I enclosed a picture, hoping an attractive blond would be enough of a reason to approve me.

Somewhat surprisingly, it worked. I received a short note back in the self-addressed envelope I'd enclosed informing me he would enjoy meeting me to discuss the finer details of drug operations.

I showed up at the prison on visitation day. I gave my name to the guard, was thoroughly searched and placed at a table to wait for Peterman. The room was large, with cafeteria style tables and chairs around it. There were several prisoners at different tables visiting with their families or friends. Looking around, I saw security cameras covering the room and suspected it might be set up for audio recordings as well. I'd have to be sure to not say anything suspicious.

A few minutes later, Peterman was led to our table where he was cuffed to a restraint anchored below the table.

"Thanks for seeing me," I opened.

"Don't get many visitors, so I'm happy you came," he smiled politely. "Make it fast though 'cause we only have fifteen minutes."

I asked a few questions about drug running, and he was happy to provide answers. He gave me more detail than I needed, but his talking made it easier for me since I really didn't care to ask a bunch of questions. Exactly fifteen minutes later, the guard returned to collect Peterman. I stood and nodded to him as I said, "Thanks for seeing me."

He smiled brightly and replied, "Any time."

As I turned to go, I looked back and asked, "Why did you kill that cop?"

My question didn't even phase him. He answered, "Wrong place at the wrong time."

I don't think I'll ever forget how little he cared about killing the love of my life.

As I reached the exit, Peterman shouted, "Come back soon!" I gave a slight wave of my hand. He likely thought I was acknowledging his request. I was really saying goodbye, knowing I'd never see him alive again.

A week later, it was announced Peterman had died from a ruptured aneurism on his brain stem. He was lucky, it was a pretty painless way to go.

CHAPTER 10

Much to my disappointment, the nightmares continued. I was unable to sleep for more than a few hours a night and knew it had to stop.

I called Father Grayson, asking if he could see me that day. His schedule was open for a few hours in the afternoon. We agreed I would come by at 2pm.

At the appointed time, I walked into the church and saw the good father waiting for me. He smiled and motioned for me to follow. We were once again seated in the confessional.

"Before we begin, will the same privacy rules be in place?" I asked.

"Of course. Every time we are seated here, you can be assured that all privacy will be maintained. Now, tell me how you are, and what I can do for you."

"I'm not well, though thank you for asking. I've been unable to sleep for weeks because of terrible nightmares."

"Have you executed anyone since our last discussion?" He asked, though I'm sure he knew the answer.

"Yes," I confirmed.

"Why did you do so?"

"He killed my boyfriend by shooting him in the face with a shotgun," I said, my voice rising slightly.

"I see. That was quite a tragedy indeed. I understand the detective was a fine man."

"Best man I ever met," I confirmed.

"I read that the prisoner died from an aneurism. You did that?"

"Yes."

"Did your boyfriend know what you do?"

"No, and long story short, I broke up with him a couple of years ago because I couldn't stand the thought of him finding out some day. It would've destroyed him."

"You said he was your boyfriend, not your ex-boyfriend. Did you reconcile?"

"Yes, about a month before he died," I nodded, a tear rolling down my cheek.

"Why did you reconcile? Did something change?"

"I changed, Father. I was happy again, and at peace. Even though I never said the words to myself, I was never going to kill again." I'd lost both the love of my life, and the will to fight my darker side. More tears followed.

Father Grayson allowed me to compose myself before continuing his questions. "You got there once; don't you think you can again?"

"I don't know, maybe that's why I'm here now."

"Can we take a step back?" he asked. "I need to understand your talents better. How are you able to give people heart attacks and aneurisms? Is there a drug that can cause these things? Something that isn't tested for during an autopsy?"

It was time for me to confess all to the father. "Father, I'm going to tell you a lot of things about myself. You probably won't believe me, but I will prove the truth to you afterwards. Please don't interrupt me, because I have a lot to say and want to get it all out."

"Take as much time as you need," came his gentle response.

Taking a deep breath, I started my explanation.

"When I was going through puberty at age thirteen, I developed headaches that were so severe, I had to go to the hospital. At first, I was diagnosed with migraines, but I didn't have nausea or light sensitivity, and the medicine they gave me didn't work at all. The doctor at the hospital ordered a CT scan of my brain. When it was read, there was a dark spot on my brain that couldn't be identified. Experts were called in and nobody knew what to make out of it. The decision was made to do an MRI the next day."

I was remembering how fearful my Dad was, and how he tried to show me a brave face. I started to cry again. "That night, my headache went away. I felt good, in fact, perfectly normal again. They did the MRI anyway, and it came back totally normal. The doctors told us the CT scan must have shown a shadow because of an error and I was discharged to normal activities."

"This is where it gets weird, Father. From that point of time, I had the ability to look at a person, and when I concentrated, I was able to see inside of them. I could literally see organs, veins, arteries, or whatever I wanted to see. And it was like x-ray vision, I was able to see these things in 3D just like normal eyesight."

I let that sink in, expecting an interruption, but Father Grayson remained silent. "At first, I couldn't control it, so I practiced. I looked inside every person I saw, until it was second nature and didn't take much effort at all. Then the biggest problem was I didn't know what most of the things I saw were. So, I got every anatomy and biology book I could find. I studied day and night until I knew what each body part was. Mind you, this took years, but by the time I was 18, I could identify problems through my sight for anyone that was within 10 feet of me. Over the years, I learned to do it for anyone within 30 feet or so."

I stopped, figuring this would be a good time to prove my claims.

"Father, I looked you over the first time we met. You only have one kidney and you have three stones in your remaining kidney. Were you aware of the stones?"

"No, I wasn't," he replied. "But you are correct about my missing kidney. I donated it to my brother when we were younger."

"You also have a small cataract developing in your right eye. I don't think it'll be a problem for a while, but you should probably see an optometrist if you have one."

"Thank you. Please continue."

"When I was eighteen, I killed my first man. It was unintentional, however. I saw a man with an almost complete blockage in his left main coronary artery. You've probably heard of widow maker heart attacks. They happen when the artery becomes 100% blocked. Widow maker heart attacks are almost always fatal, unless emergency care can be provided immediately."

I remembered the day so clearly. I wanted to help the man and was sure I could do it. I shook my head and continued, "I thought I might be able to manipulate the clot to free up the blood flow. When I was younger and experimenting with my gift, I'd learned I could not only see issues, I could manipulate tissue. The first time I did it was on myself. I'd cut my finger at school, a simple paper cut. I looked at the tissue and willed it back together. It healed right in front of my eyes."

I paused, collecting my thoughts. "It made me feel powerful, special. And at that age, I didn't handle it well. I started healing other people when they had small problems. It was easy for me, but at some point, I realized I needed to better hide my talents and I stopped. But when I saw this man, I just knew I could help him. Because of my past successes and in my arrogance, I went ahead and freed the clot. Unfortunately, the clot moved further along the artery, became stuck again and resulted in a 100% blockage. The man died from a heart attack right in front of me. I didn't know what to do, so I ran away."

Tears came to my eyes as I recalled my terrible error. I took a moment to settle down before continuing. "I decided I would go to medical school. Not necessarily to be a practicing physician, but because I wanted to make sure I never hurt anyone again when I was trying to help them." I paused for a breath.

"May I ask questions now?"

"Fire away," I said.

"How do you kill using your gift?"

I caught his use of the word 'gift' and knew that would come into the discussion later.

"I'm able to create complete blockages wherever I want them to be. I can also manipulate tissue when needed to create other conditions."

"Are you able to see things like tumors or cancer?"

"Yes, but I don't think I can cure them."

"What about viral or bacterial infections," Father Grayson asked.

"No. All I can see is how tissue has been impacted by the infections."

This time it was the Father who paused. He finally said, "There are numerous examples of healers throughout history. In the Catholic Church for example, we have Saints, like Padre Pio who performed miracle healings. There are other examples, like John of God, who have allegedly been able to heal people. I guess my point is, God gives people blessings and I'm sure he gave you his blessing for you to help and heal, not kill."

I couldn't really argue with him. Down deep, I knew I was wrong to take matters into my own hands.

"What can I do Father?"

"Why don't you use your gift to help others?"

"I do when I can. Whenever I see something that I can explain based on my medical background, I tell people they need to get checked out. I also have helped intervene with small things like accidents to help the injured. What else can I do?" I asked plaintively.

"The church has a monthly free checkup day, where physicians donate their time to help anyone who stops by. Mostly they are checking blood pressure, looking at sore throats and the like. Why don't you volunteer?" he asked.

"I'd love to, but I'm not a practicing physician. I can't legally offer medical services without a license."

"What if you were a volunteer, greeting people at the door and directing them to the correct location? You could screen them, then tell me if you see anything of importance. I'll tell our physician volunteers to look carefully for whatever the issue is."

"But what about something internal, like cancer, that is not yet presenting itself in a visible way?" I asked.

"Then I'll tell the person the Lord is working through our clinic and tell them exactly what they need to know. I promise I will never reveal the source of the information."

I wasn't comfortable with his suggestion. I'd been hiding for so long, it was contrary to my nature to put myself in such a vulnerable position. The more I considered it though, the more I liked being able to help people. "Deal, but I will only work one day to see how it goes. If it's a success, I'll happily do it again."

"Thank you," he said. "Is there anything else I need to know?"

"I don't think so. I'm pretty sure I'll sleep well again."

Father Grayson gave me the details for the next clinic day and blessed me once again before I left. Sure enough, sleep came easily and untroubled from that point forward.

CHAPTER 11

The first clinic day was two Saturdays after my second confession. Upon arrival, I received instructions on my role. Three physicians were working that day, a pediatric specialist, a general practitioner and an internal medicine doctor. I would greet each person who came, then direct them to the waiting area for the proper physician. Father Grayson would always stay near the front in case I saw something of importance.

The entire morning went by without anyone presenting with a serious concern. While I'd never heard of this monthly service, it appeared the public knew it well. I estimated over 50 people came through in the first few hours. The worst thing I saw was significant lung damage from smoking, and since the patient was using an oxygen bottle, it was no secret.

The afternoon was a bit different. While traffic slowed noticeably, the severity picked up. One gentleman who appeared to be in his forties had a serious melanoma on his back. I could not find that it had spread though, so with a clean removal, he would be fine. I nodded to the Father, telling him about the spot. Father spoke with the internal medicine physician, who investigated the patient's back and referred him to a dermatologist.

The next gentleman who concerned me had significant blockage in his right coronary artery. It was the type of blockage that could be handled relatively easily if dealt with now but would create real problems if the patient waited.

Once again, I whispered details to the Father and directed the patient to the internal medicine waiting area. Later I learned the patient did confirm occasional tightness in his chest and shortness of breath. He was sent straight to the hospital for testing.

By the end of the day, I was tired but happy. Helping people was a lot more rewarding than offing them. I spent the rest of the night singing to myself as I cleaned my condo.

I also called Becky, setting up brunch for Sunday. We were there for two hours, having a blast, laughing at each other and our lame jokes. Becky's new favorite blond joke, of which she had many to make fun of me, went like this:

A blonde female police officer pulled over a blond female driver for running a red light. When the officer walked up to the driver's window, she asked the driver for her license. The blonde driver looked around her purse, finally confessing she didn't know what the license was, so the driver asked the officer what it looked like. The officer replied that it was square and had her picture on it. The blonde driver rummaged through her purse again, finding a square mirror. She looked at it and handed it to the blonde officer.

After looking at the mirror, the officer said, "Never mind, you can go. I didn't realize you were a police officer also."

It was so silly, we both died laughing. I suspect some of the other diners thought we were drunk on mimosas.

Monday arrived and it was back to work. Late morning the business line rang. Lee was on the other line, so I answered.

"Edwards' Investigations, how may I help you?"

"Jessie Edwards please." The caller was male, with a crisp, unaccented diction.

"Speaking," I replied.

"Ms. Edwards, my name is Robert Jones. I would like to meet with you to discuss employing your services."

"That would be fine, when would you like to come by?"

"I'd prefer if you would come to my office," he replied, adding, "I'm in downtown New Orleans."

I drummed my fingers on the desktop, while considering what to say. "I generally don't make house calls," I finally replied.

"Part of the discussion involves some things I have here to show you. It really would be easier for you to come to me," he replied.

"I guess I can do that. When would you like to meet?"

"Excellent. How does your schedule look tomorrow?"

"I'm free before noon, but busy the rest of the day," I replied.

"Let's meet at my office at 9am then."

After I agreed, he provided me the necessary information.

Tuesday morning found me outside a non-descript office building in New Orleans. The office I was looking for was on the top floor. The sign on the door read, "TAM Enterprises."

The door was locked, but a buzzer with a sign was beside the door. The sign instructed visitors to ring the bell. Upon doing so, a feminine voice replied, "Can I help you?"

"My name is Jessie Edwards. I have an appointment with Robert Jones."

"Please come in," and the door buzzed, unlocking for me to enter. The office suite looked to be a standard set up, with a small reception area and individual offices lining the walls I could see. A smartly dressed woman in her fifties escorted me to a well-appointed conference room. She brought me a coffee and told me Robert would be in shortly.

A tall, fit and very attractive man walked in with a smile on his face. He extended his hand to me. As I stood to take it, he introduced himself. "I'm Robert Jones, thank you for coming."

"My pleasure," I replied, returning to my seat. As he sat, I asked, "TAM Enterprises? I haven't heard of the company."

He smiled. "I'm not surprised. We're with the federal government, a sub-branch of the Central Intelligence Agency."

"What could the CIA possibly want from a small Louisiana investigation company?" I asked, confused and concerned.

"Not so much with your company, more with you," he said.

"Then what would the CIA want with me?" I had a growing suspicion I wasn't going to like where this conversation led, but I was going to stick it out and learn what I needed to know.

"Before I answer that, let me give you a little background. My division is the Threat Analysis and Mitigation division. TAM for short, hence the name on the door. Our division is charged with identifying threats that may affect the interests of the United States at some point in the future, then doing whatever we can to reduce or eliminate the threat. We don't do wet work; our work is much more subtle." He paused, "Any questions so far?"

I had a million but wanted to get as much out of him as possible first, so I shook my head.

He continued, "There are a lot of bad guys out there. Some of them get assassinated, and some don't. But any time a public figure gets assassinated, there are repercussions in the international community. Hence our division. If we can identify potential areas of problems, and eliminate them without messy assassinations, everyone is better off."

"Makes sense to me, but I still don't see how I can be of service," I said, now certain things were going downhill fast.

Robert picked up a remote, lowered the window shades, turned off the lights and turned on a projector. On the screen was an image of Senator Guidry at the podium outside the courthouse in New Orleans.

"Recognize this?" Robert asked.

"Senator Guidry," I replied evenly.

The next slide was a security camera image of me bumping into Gary Bordelon at the courthouse. "What about this?"

"Yeah, he's the guy that killed Madison Reynolds."

Robert clicked the control and the next image appeared. It was of me sitting across the table from Eric Peterman in prison. They had made a connection, so it just remained to be seen how much shit would hit the fan.

"And this," he asked.

"Doing some research," I replied nonchalantly.

Robert left the image up, while staring me down. "Let's not play games. You're a killer, and a really good one at that. I haven't been able to figure out how you do it, but I admire your work."

"I don't know what you're talking about," I stated flatly.

"Of course you don't, but let's say for the moment I'm right. Your talent is exactly what we're looking for. Terrible people dying from heart attacks or aneurisms. No muss, no fuss and it all looks natural. It's fucking genius."

"Does seem like a tidy solution, too bad I can't help you." It was time for me to extract myself. "Thanks for inviting me, but it's obvious we don't have anything further to talk about." I turned to leave, when Robert intervened.

"Ms. Edwards, I strongly advise you to hear me out. There would be tremendous benefits to the United States, and of course your compensation would be of the highest caliber."

"I'm not interested in your money, Mr. Jones."

"Let me ask you, were you aware Senator Guidry was innocent when you killed him?" The question was like a kick in the ribs, but I knew I couldn't let him see me react. My face never flinched as I said, "I didn't kill him, I read it was a heart attack. And he had already been found innocent, so what's your point?"

"My point is this: You kill people whom you believe have escaped justice. You've been seen at the scene of quite a few suspiciously timed deaths. Too many to be a coincidence. Would you like to review the images and videos of you with the people you killed to refresh your memory?"

Part of me wanted to say 'yes' to see what he really had, but good sense overruled that impulse. "No thanks. I haven't killed anyone, so no need for you to show me anything else."

"Doesn't it bother you to have murdered an innocent man?"

Fuck Yes it did, but I knew I couldn't let on, so I didn't reply.

He added, "It would bother me if I terminated an innocent man. I'm sure of that."

I wanted to puke from the revelation. "The jury found him not guilty, even though the evidence was pretty compelling. Why do you think he was innocent?" I asked, wanting to see where I'd gone wrong.

"We were working a case involving Russian interference with elections. We captured a Russian national who'd broken into the Senator's office to plant bugs. During our interrogation, he spilled that the senator had been framed by other Russian operatives. He gave enough detail for us to confirm his story was probably true. With the Senator going on trial, and since we couldn't reveal what we knew or how we knew it, we arranged for the jury to find him not guilty. Trust me when I tell you that's no easy feat nowadays."

He did seem to be pleased with himself as he continued, "We captured the operatives involved and arranged an exchange with Russia to get a couple of our guys back." The knot in my stomach was getting worse, but I forged ahead.

"And if I could do the things you're describing, what would you want from me?"

"To quietly make troublemakers go away," he said with finality.

I nodded, not sure how to proceed. After a moment, I said, "I need to think on it. Call me next week."

"Fair enough," he said, standing and extending his hand.

I clasped his hand and left the office without another word. The first part of the drive back to the office was spent going through all the evidence I remembered in the Guidry case. I never had a doubt about his guilt and my error led to the death of an innocent man. I thought about his poor kids, now without their mother or father, and half of it was my fault. I cried the rest of the way back across Lake Ponchartrain.

I desperately needed to speak with Father Grayson. He didn't answer so I left a message, asking when he would have time for me to visit. Five minutes after I got back, Father Grayson returned my call. He confirmed any time after 7pm he would be available. I told him I would stop by at 7.

Once at the church, I told Father it was time for another confession. We adjourned to the booth.

"It's good to see you, Jess. The people you helped at clinic have all done very well. I think you've found your calling," he said brightly.

"I'm glad Father. It was nice to help people for a change."

"What has you troubled?"

"I received a call from a government agency telling me they would like to hire me. I thought they were looking for a PI, but turns out, they know about me."

When I said this, Father Grayson stiffened in his chair, and alarm sounded in his voice as he asked, "How could they know?"

"They have a lot of photos and videos with me around people who died suddenly. Too many to be a coincidence in their words. They can't figure out how I did it, and that impressed them to the point they want to hire me to help with some of their problems."

"What agency is it?"

"It's a sub-department of the CIA," I replied. "It focuses on preventing situations from escalating in the future. My talents would be particularly helpful since the deaths I'm involved in appear to be the result of natural causes. The agency doesn't like messy assassinations; there are too many political concerns in play."

"What are you going to do?" He asked quietly.

I shrugged my shoulders, "I don't think I can do it. Ever since I've stopped, I've found peace. And helping those people made me feel good, really good. It was like I finally found my calling as you said. I just can't imagine going back to my old life now."

"Then it's settled," Father Grayson declared.

"Maybe, but that's not the biggest reason I'm here."

"Go on," he prompted.

"When Senator Guidry died at the podium, that was my work," I said. "During the meeting, I found out he was innocent. He'd been framed by Russians. The agency found out about it, caught the guys who framed him, and traded them for American operatives."

I didn't say anything else, so Father finished the sentiment. "You killed an innocent man, then."

Tears came again, my sobbing was his confirmation.

Minutes went by with me crying, and Father remaining silent. The weight of killing an innocent man crushed me as surely as if a ton of bricks had fallen on me. I kept telling myself, 'Rule number two, rule number two,' over and over. I had failed to follow my rules again.

Father Grayson finally broke the silence, "Jessie, the truth can't be

91

sugar-coated. You take this risk every time you execute a person. No matter how sure you are, you may not be right. Are you still willing to risk killing innocent people." I hung my head in shame and defeat.

The nightmares returned that night. Peaceful sleep was non-existent for the next week. I became short with both Lee and Becky. Bad enough that they quit talking to me unless it was absolutely necessary.

The following Tuesday, Robert called the office to get my answer. I told him I wouldn't be able to help and hung up. On Wednesday, a package was delivered to the office. In it was a folder containing documents and photographs of a suicide bombing in Iraq. A child had detonated a suicide vest, killing himself and two soldiers when it exploded. There was nothing else contained within the package. Robert was trying to get my attention.

Thursday, he called again.

"Did you receive my folder?" He asked.

"I did. Terrible stuff, but I'm still not interested."

Before I could hang up again, he persisted. "Don't hang up. Please hear me out."

"You've got two minutes."

"In western Iraq, there's a refugee camp loosely watched by the Iraqi army, but not really under anyone's control. There are quite a number of orphans in the camp as a result of the war. The orphans attend a school run by a cleric, Mohammed Issa. Issa is thought to have been involved with ISIS, but no definitive proof was ever obtained. What we do know is Issa's indoctrinating these kids. He's championing martyrdom, while railing against the infidels. The kid who blew up two of our soldiers came from that school."

He paused to let that sink in. "This is the type of situation that needs your talents. A quiet, natural death would never cause a ripple, but if we went in and assassinated him, Issa would be forever revered, and those kids would likely be pushed further down the path of martyrdom, because we would have confirmed all Issa has been teaching them."

I was about to interrupt, but he had one last thing to say. "It's in your power to make sure none of those kids die needlessly."

That was a fucking low blow. Before hanging up on him, I said, "I'll get back to you."

I didn't pass 'go', I didn't collect two hundred bucks, I immediately drove to the church. Father Grayson was busy and asked me to come back in two hours. I sat in the waiting area instead.

Once back in the confessional, I regurgitated the facts as presented and asked, "If you could stop these kids from becoming suicide bombers by killing one man, would you do it?"

"I would not because I don't think it's ever permitted to kill. The commandment is very clear on that. Even so, the Old Testament endorsed war against tribes who killed their children. These tribes were sacrificing children to their gods, Baal and Molech. God found this so offensive, war was permitted to eliminate this practice. 2 Kings 23:10 reads, 'He defiled Topeth, which is in the valley of the son of Hinnon, that no man might make his son or daughter to pass through the fire unto Molech.' He as referenced in the passage was King Josiah of Judah."

Father continued, "Leviticus has several passages regarding this as well. One that comes to mind is Leviticus 20:2. It reads, 'Again, thou shalt say to the children of Israel, Whoever he be of the children of Israel, or of the strangers that sojourn to Israel, that giveth any of his seed unto Molech; he shall surely be put to death: the people of the land shall stone him with stones.' A strict interpretation of these passages certainly condones killing to prevent children from being sacrificed to Molech."

I pondered the information. "It seems God has a soft place for children."

"Yes, He does," Father acknowledged.

Back in my car, I called Robert. "That was fast," he said.

"It's time to go Old Testament," I replied.

"Not sure what that means. Are you in?"

"Yes, I'll come see you tomorrow. I want to get everything straight."

"Be here at 9am." I acknowledged and hung up. Maybe saving innocent people would help me atone for my sins.

CHAPTER 12

t the appointed time, I was seated in Robert's office.

"I'm glad you came around. Your help will save a lot of people," he said.

"We need to get some things straight before I agree." He nodded, so I continued, "First, I only take cases that I approve of. I reserve the right to reject any request."

He made a note on his iPad. "Second, the fee is two million per assignment, half up front and the rest upon completion."

He asked, "Will you want this paid to your company or an offshore account?"

"Neither. You'll open a trust account at St. Jude's Hospital in honor of Madison Reynolds. The only payment to my company is $1000 per day for each day I work. That's my standard rate."

"Agreed," he said.

"Last, you will never ask how I do what I do. And I'll need that confirmed with your bosses before I agree."

"I don't see that as a problem," he said, making a note again. He rose from his chair, saying, "If you'll excuse me, I need to make a call."

I nodded and out he went. Five minutes later, he returned saying, "We have a deal." I shook his hand to seal it, wondering what I'd gotten myself into.

"How's this Issa problem going to be handled?" I asked.

"The United Nations has aid workers at the camp. We'll fly you to Baghdad where you will meet with your handler, Sami Kolh. He goes by 'Sam'. He's an Iraqi national we've worked with for about ten years. Sam will act as your guide and interpreter. His job is to make sure you get to the camp safely, help you to find Issa, and then get you back to Baghdad once you've completed the mission. We don't care how you do it, just make sure it's natural causes. Any questions?"

"Where's the camp?"

"It's outside a town named Anah in western Iraq, not too far from the Syrian border."

"Will I be traveling under my own name?"

"No. You'll have an alias set up with appropriate paperwork to make sure you have no difficulties getting into and out of any country."

Robert went on to explain the remaining details to me over the next half hour. It was obvious he was a professional and knew his business.

When he was done, I asked, "When would I need to leave?"

"Sunday at the latest," he replied.

"And you can get my new identity set up that fast?"

Robert just looked at me, cocking his head to the side as if to say, 'that's a dumb question.'

"Never mind," I said. "How long do you anticipate I'll be gone?"

"Up to 14 days, depending on how things go once you get there."

Pulling out my phone, I looked at my calendar. The next two weeks had quite a few appointments, but all were able to be rescheduled. "Okay, let's make it happen. Don't forget, I don't go anywhere until I verify one million dollars has been set up in a trust at St. Jude's."

"It'll be done by the end of the day," he stated with confidence.

"I'll be calling them tomorrow to confirm. If it's not there, you know what happens," I said resolutely.

"Understood."

I excused myself knowing lots of work had to be done to get me on a flight in two days. I called Lee and told him I'd be out of town for two weeks starting Sunday. He asked if everything was okay. I told him all was well, I just had to do a job for the government and couldn't share the details. He was instructed to reschedule my appointments accordingly.

I then called Becky, asking if she could meet for dinner. I wanted to let her know I'd be gone for a while. I also wanted to apologize for my recent poor attitude. She agreed, so we confirmed a time and a restaurant for that evening. The rest of the day flew by as I made the other preparations. Everything from holding mail, to paying bills had to be done. Tedious stuff for sure, but important nonetheless.

By the time dinner arrived, I was ready for a cocktail. Seated with drinks in hand, I raised my glass and said, "Cheers."

We clinked glasses and sipped our drinks. The bourbon went down smoothly, settling comfortably in my stomach.

"I want to apologize for my behavior the past couple of weeks. I've allowed stress to affect my behavior, and I'm sorry. You don't deserve that."

She nodded, "Apology accepted. What's been going on?"

"Unusual work stress has me down, but I'm dealing with it," I replied. "I'm also going out of town on a job for about two weeks so wanted to see you," I added.

"Where to?"

"I can't really say, but it's a long way from here." I knew she would think that meant another state.

"That's cool, you going to be able to sightsee a little?"

"I expect so. Should be an interesting trip," I replied.

"Make sure to take some pictures."

"Sure thing. What's been going on in your world?" I asked, wanting to move away from my upcoming mission.

Since we hadn't been getting together as often as I'd like, it was nice to catch up on Becky's life. We traded stories about our daily existences, ate a wonderful meal and spent a lot of time talking about the little things that made us happy. It was a perfect evening with my best friend.

On the way home, I called Lee. I apologized to him for my behavior. He hadn't deserved the way I'd treated him either.

The next day was spent researching where I was going and packing the essentials. I remembered to call St. Jude. They confirmed a one-million-dollar deposit had been made on behalf of Madison.

Robert told to report to Belle Chase Naval Air Base at 8:30am Sunday. With the flight time and time difference, I'd be landing at Ramstein AFB around 11:00pm local time. My flight to Iraq was scheduled to take off seven hours later. With Baghdad being only an hour ahead of Germany, my internal clock shouldn't be disrupted too much by the trip. At least, that's what I was hoping.

Arriving the next morning at Belle Chase Naval Base, I found Robert waiting for me at the security gate. He got us through and escorted me to a Lear jet parked on the tarmac.

"Nothing but the best for you," he smiled, motioning towards the jet.

"I expect five-star dining, too," I laughed.

"But of course, Mademoiselle," he replied in a surprisingly good French accent. "Caviar and champagne await you."

I laughed again as he escorted me onto the plane. Once aboard, Robert went through the mission details, documents and supplies, which included a pistol. I was a proficient shooter, having learned with both Becky and Sam. Even so, I didn't want the gun.

"No guns," I said after the inventory check was complete.

"You sure?" Robert asked. "It's a dangerous place you're going."

"UN aid personnel don't carry weapons, and I don't want one either."

"Your call," he acceded. We then went over my cover. My name was Leslie Truman. I was a nurse from New Orleans on my first trip abroad. We carefully went through the background story, before he handed me a detailed dossier on my new self with instructions to learn it forward and backwards. The last thing Robert did was hand me a satellite phone. He told me it was for emergencies. With the briefing completed, I settled in for the ten-hour flight to Germany. Between studying, a couple of movies, some stretching and a long nap, the trip passed much quicker than I thought it would.

After landing in Germany, I decided I would add a requirement to any future jobs; travel must be by Lear Jet.

I was met at the steps by Major Tidwell. He escorted me to my quarters, explained the layout of the facility and cautioned me to stay in the room, except for bathroom breaks. He told me I would be awakened at 4:30am to get ready for the flight. Despite my nerves, I was able to sleep a few hours before the knock came at my door. When all was in order, I was escorted to a huge plane. I asked the major about it. He told me it was a Boeing C-17 Globemaster. I was the only passenger on the flight, since the plane was being used to deliver supplies for troops stationed in Baghdad. The major told me I could sit anywhere, and the flight would be about 5 hours long.

Accommodations were sparse compared to the Lear, but comfortable enough for the shorter flight. It was clear caviar and champagne would not be on the menu though. I spent most of the time reviewing my background and mission details. I looked over Issa's picture carefully, making sure I knew his face well.

Leslie Truman exited the flight at Baghdad International Airport.

The plane had taxied to a set of hangers not associated with commercial travel. At the bottom of the ramp waiting for me was Sami.

"Hi Miss Truman," Sami said in excellent English. "I'm Sami, but feel free to call me Sam."

I shook his hand, replying, "If it's okay, I'd prefer calling you Sami." He smiled his agreement before escorting me to a red Kia Sportage sitting outside the security fence. Sami loaded my bag and equipment in the back, before climbing in the driver's seat.

Starting the car, he said, "We'll lay low today, so you can rest and recover from your journey. The convoy is scheduled to leave tomorrow morning at six. We will be escorted by a contingent of Iraqi regulars until we reach Anah. Its about 350 kilometers to Anah and usually takes 5 hours or so. The refugee camp is a few kilometers out of town."

"I'm feeling pretty good, Sami. Can we do a little sightseeing instead of resting?"

"This area is as safe as it's been for years, so I don't see why not," he replied. "Do you like museums?"

"Absolutely!" I exclaimed. "The World War II Museum in my hometown of New Orleans is one of my favorite places to visit."

"Wonderful," he replied. "We have two excellent ones here. The Iraq Museum and the Baghdadi Museum. You'll learn much about the area today."

We spent the next six hours touring the museums, and true to Sami's word, it was a wonderful way to learn more about the region's rich history. We stayed at a small hotel in the International Zone that night. Morning found us waiting at the staging area for the convoy. Though I'd worn western attire the day before, today I was dressed in the Hijab, long sleeves and a long skirt. I wanted to be prepared for my time in the conservative, rural areas we would be traveling through and to.

About twenty aid workers were loaded in a bus for transport. With no air conditioning, I was happy the November temperatures were mild. The bus was accompanied by several supply trucks and a contingent of 10 or so Iraqi soldiers. We introduced ourselves to members of the aid team, finding out that the workers came from a wide variety of countries around the world.

During the ride, I questioned Sami about what to expect. He told me the refugee camp was kept away from Anah out of respect for the villagers' wishes. He explained that during the Gulf War, Anah remained independent by not allowing tribal factions to exert control, and even the US forces had agreed to remain outside of the city.

Iraqi troops came to the camp a couple of times a month, but all other times, the camp was left to its own devices. That's what allowed Issa to exert the influence he had over the children.

Sami showed me a rough diagram of the camp, about 5 kilometers southeast of Anah. It looked larger than I expected, prompting me to inquire about the number of refugees. He said the best estimates put the number around 10,000 people, making it much larger than I anticipated. There were a few permanent buildings, but most structures were more temporary in nature.

The quarters for the aid workers were in the southernmost portion of the camp. The school was in the western part of the camp. Sami told me because of the camp's size, and Issa's schedule, we may not see Issa for a while. He previously asked me how close I needed to be to do my job. I had told him it would be ideal if I could be in the same room as Issa.

The trip through the flat, dry plain was bumpy, but uneventful. Upon arriving at the camp, the bus was directed to the UN worker section, while the supply trucks went to make their deliveries. A senior staffer gave us directions to our assigned bunks, with mine being in a tent reserved for female workers. Sami's tent was a couple of hundred yards to the west of mine. In the middle of the "housing" area, a metal building had been erected. It served as both our mess hall and meeting room.

We'd arrived at lunchtime, receiving instructions to stow our gear and assemble in the lunchroom for food and orientation. The food was exactly what you'd expect; warm and tasteless. With the windows opened, the building had a nice breeze blowing through keeping us comfortable.

With lunch done, the new workers were kept for orientation. The senior staffer who met us at the bus walked to the front of the room.

"Good afternoon. My name is Rory McCord. I'm the Team Leader for this humanitarian undertaking. Thank you for your willingness to help others who are in dire need. Your time here will not be easy, but it will be rewarding. The refugees at the camp mostly come from Syria, victims of the civil war. There are some Iraqis as well. They were victims of the ISIS caliphate that was centered in western Iraq. Many of these refugees are children, with almost 100 of these children being orphans.

Rory looked around the room, making sure to make eye contact with each person. "Our job here sounds simple: we are here to provide assistance to the refugees until they can be settled in a permanent location. Assistance comes in several forms, from food and housing, to medical care and even education. Each of you has been assigned to one of those areas for support. A roster is posted over here," he said pointing to a bulletin board. "Your assignments are noted, as is your primary service location. Beside the roster, you'll see a map of the camp. Take a picture of it and keep it with you. It's easy to get lost around here until you learn your way around."

"Are there any questions before I go through the rules?" He looked around, but nobody raised their hands.

"First rule is, do not go out at night unless your job requires it. The mess hall is open until 9pm local time to provide meals for workers getting off later in the evening. If you are one of those workers, go straight back to your bunk upon leaving. Do not wander about the camp."

He paused to emphasize that point. "This area is not entirely secure. There are occasional bandits, mostly made up of former ISIS fighters. They come to steal supplies from time to time. Do not confront any armed person at all, ever. Understood?" We all nodded.

"The next rule is for the women. You will need to dress in local traditional attire. This means you should always wear a Hijab in public, as well as long sleeves and pants or a long skirt. Show as little skin as possible. I know this doesn't conform to your usual attire, but we must do this in order to make sure we are not creating controversy while here." This wasn't a problem as Robert had provided appropriate dress for me.

"Our third rule is for the women again. Never be alone with a local or refugee man without another male UN worker present. We staff each service to allow for this so it shouldn't be difficult to follow this rule. If you're out and come across a local, do not engage in conversation. I recommend lowering your head and looking away. I know this sound harsh, but it's the reality we are working in. Questions?"

I raised my hand and was acknowledged. "What should we do if a man speaks to us during an encounter, and a male worker is not present?"

"Do you speak Arabic?"

"No," I answered.

"Then it's easy. Most of the refugees don't know English. Just walk away, moving towards any area where there are people. We have translators available at all the stations so language should not be a barrier to your work. Any other questions?"

Another woman asked, "Are there soldiers here to protect us?"

Rory sighed, "There are supposed to be, but the army has been less than efficient in this regard. We see troops sporadically, but they're not here much of the time."

CHAPTER 13

The meeting ended, with everyone returning to their bunks. My tent had four beds in it, one with linens folded at the base of the bed and the other three made up. I unloaded my bag into a footlocker that was beside the unmade bed and pulled up the picture of the camp map. I wanted to memorize where my points of interests were in relation to each other. I noted the women's bath and shower facility was only two stops down from my tent. That was going to make it convenient when getting ready for bed or to start my day.

While studying the map, a knock sounded on the doorframe.

"Come in," I said, looking to see who was at the door.

Sami peered in, his eyes adjusting from the brightness of the day. "Settled in?" He asked.

"Really not much to do, so yes?" I laughed

He chuckled as well. "I thought we would walk around the camp this afternoon. We may get lucky and catch sight of Issa." Checking out the area made sense as I wasn't scheduled to be in the medical facility until the next day.

"Lead the way," I said, gesturing to the door.

Once outside, I suggested we go to the school first. No point in waiting if I could get lucky the first day. It took about ten minutes to get to the school. The building was a permanent structure, though small. As we approached, the call to prayer went out across loudspeakers.

People stopped their activities and went through the ritual for the afternoon prayer. Sami participated as well. I moved to the side and remained quiet.

With the late afternoon prayer completed, activity returned to normal and we went to the school. The building contained one large room with desks grouped in different areas. Sami explained that children who attended class were segregated by age or ability for lessons appropriate to each one's level. There were also lectures for all students at the same time. These were frequently done by my target, Issa.

We saw twenty or thirty kids in the room, and several adults, but Issa was not one of them. We moved on, completing a tour of the camp over the next hour. By then, it was time to return to the mess hall for dinner. Seated with our treys of food, I asked, "Do you know where Issa stays?"

Sami should his head, "I do not."

"Can we ask around?"

"I wouldn't be comfortable doing so. That's the kind of attention we don't need," he replied. Though disappointed by his response, I understood his reticence.

Over the next few days, I settled into my role in the medical facility. Most of the cases we saw were simple in nature. The biggest difficulty we had was the lack of proper equipment and supplies. It seemed we were short on most of the medicines we needed to treat people, even with the resupply that had come with my convoy.

The physician in charge of the clinic was from Italy. His English was good enough that we didn't have much difficulty communicating regarding treatment plans. I used my talent as much as I could, and when I saw something concerning, I did an examination that gave me the right results to help diagnose the condition correctly.

On my third day, an emergency case was brought in with a gunshot would. The bullet had entered the patient's thigh. My sight told me the bullet nicked the femoral artery. A tourniquet had been applied to the patient's leg, keeping him from bleeding out, but it needed to be released in order to prevent possible complications. Using my talent, I knitted the femoral artery back together. The bullet was now behind it, but the artery would not bleed further.

With the danger under control, I loosened the tourniquet, while keeping pressure on the entry wound. The surgical suite was prepped, and the patient taken in for bullet extraction. The surgery was successful, and the patient was expected to make a full recovery.

After the procedure, the surgeon was in the break room speaking with another doctor. I was able to overhear him discussing the case.

"It was one of the strangest wounds I've seen," he said. "The artery wasn't damaged at all, but the bullet was directly behind it. If you drew a straight line from the entry point to the final resting point of the bullet, that shouldn't be possible."

The other physician replied, "There's no big mystery, the bullet moved location during patient transit and ended up behind the artery."

The surgeon said, still shaking his head, "I guess that's what it was, but it's weird."

I smiled and took another sip of coffee.

Each day, Sami and I went to the school looking for Issa. It was hard to coordinate due to our work schedules, but we managed to make the trip at least once a day. One time, I'm pretty sure I saw him, but he was far away amongst a group of men, leaving me no chance to complete my task.

The next day marked my one-week anniversary at the camp. Routines had been established, and it was just a waiting game. I was getting nervous the longer it took, always worried about something going wrong and me being discovered as an imposter.

The supply convoy arrived around noon, bringing a few new workers, along with supplies. The soldiers went through the camp, before boarding the trucks and leaving.

It was early in my second week when all hell broke loose. It was dinnertime, and a group of workers were in the mess hall, Sami and me included. We heard loud noises and shouting coming from outside. Five men, armed with short, semi-automatic weapons burst into the hall, screaming directions in Arabic. I couldn't understand them, but their motions made it clear we were to move to the back of the hall. Sami whispered to me that these were likely ISIS fighters looking for supplies.

Our team leader took control, making sure we followed directions. Though I was scared to death, I admired his calm and collected demeanor. I could see why he had the team lead role.

After a few moments of no activity, I quietly asked Sami, "Why aren't they grabbing supplies?"

With a shake of his head, he whispered, "I don't know."

It was at that moment Issa marched in with six boys. The kids appeared to be anywhere from 10-15 years old. Issa was speaking to them loudly, while pointing at us. I looked to Sami, so he summarized for me.

Issa was telling the children we were the infidels. We weren't there to help, we were there to poison their minds and take them away from Allah. It was Allah's will that we be killed.

Nobody moved, waiting for something to happen. Issa reached behind his back and extracted a wicked looking knife from his belt. He handed it to the oldest boy, telling the boy to pick one of us to behead.

The boy looked terrified, but Issa's constant badgering led the boy to point at Sami. Two of the terrorists started our way, and Sami turned to me in horror. I said, "I'll handle this, but give me your word you'll keep your mouth shut."

Wide-eyed, he just nodded. I stared at Issa for the briefest of moments. Issa's eyes erupted from his head. He screamed and dropped to his knees, grabbing at his bleeding eye sockets. Everyone else also started screaming, except for Issa who stopped quickly. That was because I used my power to tear his throat open, leaving him a gurgling mess, writhing on the floor.

The terrorists raised their guns, not knowing what to do. Before any trigger was pulled, each dropped to the ground clutching at their chests. I grabbed Sammi, telling him to interpret my words for the kids. I assume he did, because when Sami done translating, all the kids nodded and ran to the door.

My words whispered to Sami were, "These men have blasphemed against Allah. Allah does not wish His name to be used in connection with terrible acts of violence. Allah ended these men for their sins. Now leave and tell everyone you know what happened here. Have them come see the bodies as proof of these words."

One of the workers went and kicked the guns away from the fallen terrorists. It was pointless since I'd torn each one's aorta away from their hearts, but it showed he was still thinking. Nobody understood what had just happened, and as everyone milled around trying to make sense of it, I grabbed Sami and pulled him out the door. We went to my tent, which was thankfully empty.

Once inside, Sami asked, "What the hell was that?"

"Remember what you promised me," I replied.

"Nobody would believe me anyway, but please tell me what just happened."

"Was your life just saved?" I asked. Sami nodded, so I continued. "I did my job and nothing more. You'll report to Robert that Issa is dead, you saw him die and you checked the body afterwards to make sure. You'll tell him nothing else other than you don't know how I did it. Do you understand?

"I gave my word and will honor it," Sami acknowledged.

"I'm glad to hear that, because my life may depend on it."

CHAPTER 14

A couple of hours later, the team leader knocked on my door and inquired about my well-being. I told him I was shaken up, but doing as well as could be expected.

He then said, "I also came to compliment you on your quick thinking. In telling the kids Allah had exacted revenge for misusing His name, I'm pretty sure you scared those kids straight for the rest of their lives."

"I hope so," I replied. "I can't imagine what they're feeling having seen such an awful thing. As much trouble as I'm having with it, it's got to be ten times worse for them."

He nodded his agreement. "Do you have any idea what happened? I mean, that man's eyes popped out and his throat literally exploded. I've never even heard of anything that could explain it."

"There's nothing in my medical background that explains it either," I replied. "As crazy as it sounds, I wouldn't be surprised if there were some sort of divine intervention."

He shook his head and after a pause said, "Let me know if there's anything I can do for you."

I thanked him as he left. Picking up my bag, I pulled out the satellite phone and powered it up. It was preprogrammed to dial Robert when activated. After some moments, I heard Robert answer, "Any luck?"

"It's done and we need out. We need out now," I said urgently.

"Have you been compromised?"

"I don't think so, but it was very public. I don't want to be here until the next supply caravan comes through."

"Understood. I'll get a chopper to you in the morning. Call me back at 6am your time," and with that, he disconnected. I found Sami and gave him the information.

True to his word, Robert got us a helicopter back to Baghdad the next morning. I told everyone the night before had traumatized me to the point I needed to leave. My explanation seemed to be accepted by the group.

By the time we made it back to Baghdad, arrangements were made for my return trip. I had to stay one last night in Baghdad before catching a morning flight to Ramstein AFB.

Sami settled me in the hotel, telling me he'd return to take me to the airport in the morning. Before he left, he said, "I don't think I've properly thanked you for what you did. Please know it is my belief when one saves another's life, the person is forever indebted to the savior, that is at least until the favor can be repaid. Your secret is safe with me. I will take it to my grave."

I hugged him, thanking him for everything he'd done to help. It was only mid-afternoon, but I went to bed and slept until morning. There were no nightmares to interrupt my sleep.

The trip back was uneventful, giving much time to reflect on what I had done. I suspected a long conversation with the good Father was going to be one of the first things I did when I got settled back home.

The jet taxied into the same area where I boarded what seemed to be a lifetime ago. Standing there to greet me was Robert, briefcase in hand.

I deplaned with a cautious look, worried about the public nature of the killing. Robert smiled and gave me a big hug.

"Well done!" and before I could respond, he broke the embrace and held out his briefcase. "Seems like we have another problem for you to solve."

The End